CW00347835

THE SOLDIERS' HOMECOMING

Brett, Logan and Sam were best friends and three of the finest soldiers in the Australian SAS K9 division. But one day Sam was killed, tearing their friendship group apart and leaving Brett and Logan with memories that would haunt them for ever.

Now, back in Australia, Brett and Logan are adjusting to life outside the army. But they haven't counted on two gorgeous, intriguing, captivating women who swan into their lives and present them with challenges they've never faced before!

Available in March

THE RETURNING HERO

and

HER SOLDIER PROTECTOR

Available in April

Dear Reader

If you've read the first book in this series, THE RETURNING HERO, you will already be familiar with the gorgeous Logan Murdoch. He's Brett's very protective soldier friend, and it was great to revisit Brett and Jamie and give Logan his own story, too.

I've been a dog-lover all my life, and because of my affinity with canines this was a very special duet to write. I loved researching the special bonds between these strong, talented soldiers and their K9 teammates, and I like the fact that their dogs are respected members of the army in their own right. Having dogs on base has not only heavily reduced the number of United States and Australian soldiers losing their lives and limbs to improvised explosive devices, it has also boosted morale.

In this story you will meet SAS soldier Logan and his beloved dog Ranger, who are both tasked with protecting country singer Candace Evans. She is the most unlikely heroine for Logan but, as you will discover, Logan is absolutely perfect for this disillusioned celebrity. Together they learn to put their troubled pasts behind them and build a future.

I hope you enjoy Logan and Candace's love story— please do contact me to share your thoughts!

Soraya

HER SOLDIER PROTECTOR

BY
SORAYA LANE

Published in Great Britain 2014
by Mills & Boon, an imprint of Harlequin (UK) Limited,
Eton House, 18-24 Paradise Road, Richmond, Surrey, TW9 1SR

© 2014 Soraya Lane

ISBN: 978 0 263 24206 5

Harlequin (UK) Limited's policy is to use papers that are natural,
renewable and recyclable products and made from wood grown in
sustainable forests. The logging and manufacturing processes conform
to the legal environmental regulations of the country of origin.

Printed and bound in Great Britain
by CPI Antony Rowe, Chippenham, Wiltshire

Writing for Mills & Boon® is truly a dream come true for **Soraya Lane**. An avid book-reader and writer since her childhood, Soraya describes becoming a published author as 'the best job in the world', and hopes to be writing heart-warming, emotional romances for many years to come.

Soraya lives with her own real-life hero on a small farm in New Zealand, surrounded by animals and with an office overlooking a field where their horses graze.

For more information about Soraya and her upcoming releases visit her at her website, www.sorayalane.com, her blog, www.sorayalane.blogspot.com, or follow her at www.facebook.com/SorayaLaneAuthor

Recent books by Soraya Lane:

THE RETURNING HERO**
PATCHWORK FAMILY IN THE OUTBACK*
MISSION: SOLDIER TO DADDY
THE SOLDIER'S SWEETHEART
THE NAVY SEAL'S BRIDE
BACK IN THE SOLDIER'S ARMS
RODEO DADDY
THE ARMY RANGER'S RETURN
SOLDIER ON HER DOORSTEP

Bellaroo Creek!
**The Soldiers' Homecoming*

DEDICATION

As a little girl I begged frequently for a dog of my own.
Thankfully I only had to wait until my seventh birthday
before I was gifted an eight-week-old Australian
Silky Terrier named Chloe. So this book is dedicated
to my amazing parents for giving this dog-loving girl
her dream come true!

CHAPTER ONE

LOGAN MURDOCH SURVEYED the waiting crowd. After years spent serving overseas, usually in the desert and lugging an eighty-pound pack on his back, he had no intention of complaining even if he had to wait another hour for his superstar client to arrive.

"Stand by for arrival in five minutes."

He touched his earpiece as the other security expert's voice came on the line.

"Cleared for arrival in five minutes," he responded.

Logan moved down the line, checking that all the waiting fans were securely behind the low, temporary fencing. A couple of policemen were on guard, keeping an eye on the large crowd, and he had a security team ready to help if he needed them. He reached down to give his dog a pat, before moving out with one minute to go to wait for the car. Logan had already led his dog around and inside the entire perimeter to check for explosives, and now their primary objective was to get the client safely from the car into the building.

"I have a visual on the car. Stand by for immediate

arrival," he said, before talking to his dog. "Stay at heel," he commanded.

His dog knew him better than any human possibly could, and the verbal command was just procedure. One look and Ranger would know what he was thinking.

The car pulled up to the curb—jet-black with dark tinted windows—and Logan stepped forward to open the back door. He'd researched his client, knew all there was to know about her in the public domain, but nothing had prepared him for seeing her in the flesh. For the slim, tanned legs that slipped from the car, the beautiful face turned up toward him or the star power she exuded from her small frame. She was gorgeous.

"Ms. Evans," he said, holding out his hand to assist her. "Please follow me immediately through the front door. Will you be signing autographs today?"

Her eyes—big blue eyes that were as wide as saucers—met his, and she shook her head. Logan might never have met her before, but something told him she was terrified.

"Yes!" someone from inside the car barked. "Candace, you're signing autographs. Go."

Logan tightened his hold on her hand as she stepped out, and suddenly they were surrounded by flashes that seemed like bulbs exploding in front of them.

"Easy," he told Ranger, his grip on the dog's leash firm. "Let's go."

He released her only when she loosened her hold, then he walked with his palm flat against her back, his dog on his other side. If she wanted to stop to talk to fans, then that was her decision, but anything that alerted him to a potential problem? Then he'd be the one calling the shots, never mind what her manager or whoever he was wanted her to do.

"Don't leave me," she whispered just loud enough for him to hear, a tremble in her voice.

"I'm right here until you tell me to go," Logan replied, moving his body closer to hers, realizing his instincts had been right. "I've swept every inch of this place, and my dog never makes mistakes."

Logan watched her nod, before bravely squaring her shoulders and raising her hand in a wave to her fans. The flashes from the paparazzi were still in full swing, and now everyone in the crowd seemed to be screaming out to the woman they'd queued hours to meet. He'd been doubtful that she needed such high-level security, but the worry in her voice told him that maybe it had been justified.

"Candace, over here!" one girl was yelling. "Please, Candace, I love you!"

Logan steered her forward, stopping only when she did. He noticed the slight shake of her hand as she signed multiple autographs, before angling her body toward the building. He took his cue.

"Autographs are over," he announced, at the same time as the crowd started yelling again.

They walked straight toward the door, stopping for a few more fans just before they disappeared inside.

Logan touched his earpiece. "We're in the building. Secure the exits."

As the doors shut behind them, Candace collapsed against the wall, her face drained of color.

"Ms. Evans?" he asked, at her side in a heartbeat.

"I'm fine. It's just overwhelming," she muttered, resting her head back against the wall. "I didn't think I was going to be able to make the walk from the car."

Logan dropped Ranger's leash and told him to stay, before crossing the room to fill two glasses of water.

"He won't hurt me, will he?"

Logan glanced back and saw that his dog was sitting to attention, ears pricked, eyes trained on her. Ranger was looking at her as though curiosity was about to get the better of him.

"Lie down," he commanded, smiling as Ranger did as he was told. "He's a big softie and he knows his manners. The worst he'd do is lick you if I let him, and he sure seems to like the look of you."

Her smile wasn't convincing, but she did seem to relax. He passed her a glass of water, trying not to look too intently at her bright blue eyes, or the long blond curls that were falling over her breasts. In real life she was beyond stunning—much shorter than he'd have guessed, and tiny, like a doll.

"Tell me why you're so scared," he asked. "I'm guessing it's more than just the bombings that have happened around the world lately to cause a seasoned superstar like you to panic."

Candace nodded, sipping her water before passing it back to him.

"I've received threats," she told him. "The first few to my house, then a package sent to my last tour bus and another to my manager. I was fine to start with, but it's starting to get to me."

Crap. He'd guessed there was more to this story, but the fact that he was head of security and hadn't been correctly briefed was a major breach of trust from everyone involved.

Logan kept his face neutral, not wanting her to see him as anything other than trustworthy and dependable. It wasn't her fault that not all the information had been passed along—he would save his anger for someone who deserved to be blasted. *Like maybe his boss or her manager.*

"I've worked with Ranger for five tours in warzones, so there is no chance an Improvised Explosive Device is coming anywhere near you without him detecting it," Logan told her. "The only thing you have to do is make sure your people keep me fully briefed at all times. No secrets, no lies."

The smile she gave him was shy, but it lit up her face, made her eyes swim to life. "Will you stay with me until I go on? I have an interview to do soon, but I'll be in my dressing room until the show."

"Yes, ma'am." There was no way he was going to walk away when he'd finally seen her smile like that.

"I don't even know your name," she said, pushing off from the wall she'd been resting against as her entourage came down the stairs at the end of the hall, having been escorted into the building through a separate door.

"Logan," he said. "And this here is Ranger."

"Call me Candace," she told him, her eyes never leaving his as they spoke. "If you're in charge of keeping me safe, you can at least call me by my first name."

Logan smiled at Candace and picked up Ranger's

leash, before following a few steps behind her. He might have moaned about being asked to work security by the Australian Army, but this job was turning out to be a whole lot more interesting than he'd expected. She was here to perform to a sold-out crowd and help promote Australia to the rest of the world at the same time, and being her private security detail might just prove to be the most enjoyable work he'd done in his career with the SAS.

Personally enjoyable, anyway. Not to mention it was a job that wasn't going to haunt him in the middle of the night like his last few assignments.

For the first time in weeks, Candace was relaxed. The tightness in her shoulders had almost disappeared, and she wasn't on edge, looking sideways to make sure no one was following her who shouldn't be. Ever since the letters had started to arrive, she'd hardly slept and almost cancelled the last leg of her world tour, but she hated letting anyone down.

And then Logan had escorted her past the waiting crowd and into the building, and the fear and terror had slowly seeped from her body.

She'd had plenty of bodyguards over the years, usually hulking guys who could deal with any physical threat. But with the latest spate of bombings around the world and the situation with the letters, she didn't just want men capable of brute strength around her. She'd asked for the best, and it looked like she'd received him.

"We'll take it from here."

She glanced across at her manager, Billy. He always

had her best intentions at heart, or at least she hoped he did, but right now she wasn't interested in doing what she was told.

"I've actually decided I want Logan to stay with me," she said.

Eyebrows were raised in her direction, and she almost laughed at the stern expression Logan was giving them in response. She doubted that he was easily intimidated, or that anyone here would have the nerve to cross him, especially not with his fierce-looking dog at his side.

"This way," Candace said, nodding toward the room with her name on it.

He followed, dog at his side, each of his footsteps covering more ground than two of hers. It was oddly comforting having his heavy boots thumping out of rhythm with the click of her heels.

"So are you in private security now?" she asked, wondering how someone who'd served in warzones was even assigned to work with her.

He chuckled. "Would you believe me if I told you I'm still SAS, but that the Australian government was so determined to have you here to promote their new tourism campaign they decided to send me here to head the security team?"

She shook her head, pushing open her door. Logan walked past her, his dog doing what appeared to be a quick check of the room.

"You're not kidding, are you?"

"Nope. But I can't say that I mind. After years on

patrol in the middle of nowhere, it's a nice change of pace before I retire."

She sat down on the sofa and gestured for him to do the same, unsure of whether she believed him or not. "What do you feel like? Sushi? Something more substantial?"

He raised an eyebrow. "You're ordering lunch for both us?"

"Ah, yes," she said, not sure why he found that so unusual. "Unless you do something different at this time of the day in Australia?"

He shook his head, a wry grin on his face. "If you're buying lunch, then I definitely have no complaints about this gig."

"I have a bit of a ritual that I always eat Japanese food before a show. I'm thinking sashimi and miso soup, but maybe you'd like something more."

"Candace, I'm used to eating dehydrated army food when I'm working, so if you feel like sushi, I say sure."

"That settles it then. I'll order." She stood up to use the phone, ordering way more food than they'd ever consume.

Candace turned back around, eyes locking on Logan's as he met her gaze. It wasn't something she was used to—a man not intimated by meeting her, not fazed by the circus they'd confronted when he'd escorted her from her car. *She* knew that she was no one special, but men usually reacted badly to her fame or her money, and the way Logan was behaving was the complete opposite. He was just staring back at her like she was... ordinary. Although she guessed a lot of it, dealing with the crowds and stress earlier, was more to do with his training than anything else.

"Can I ask you something?"

He shrugged. "Shoot."

"You're the first guy in years who's treated me like a regular woman and not a celebrity. Is it your training or just how you are?"

He leaned back, crossing his legs at the ankle and stretching out his big body. Logan was tall and fit, the T-shirt he wore snug to his athletic frame, pants stretching over his thigh muscles. She'd sure hit the jackpot where he was concerned.

"*Aren't* you a regular woman?"

She felt a blush crawl up her neck and heat her cheeks. It had been a *long* time since a man had drawn that kind of reaction from her, but he'd said it like it was the most logical answer in the world. Which she kind of guessed it was.

"Of course I am," she said, refusing to be embarrassed. "It's just that men usually avoid me, look at me like I'm some freak show because they've seen me on television or in magazines, or otherwise they're all over me. Even most of my bodyguards have never gotten used to dealing with the whole fan and paparazzi thing."

"Sounds like you haven't spent much time with real men," he said with a chuckle. "Or maybe it's just that Australian men aren't so easily intimidated. A pretty lady is a pretty lady, no matter who she is, and at the end of the day, I'd rather a camera in my face than a semi-automatic."

He thought she was pretty? "Well, maybe I should

spend more time *down under*. Is that what you call it here?"

"Yeah, that's what we call it."

Candace could tell he was trying not to laugh.

"So, are you going to hang around for the concert?"

"Is that an invite?"

"There's a VIP pass with your name on it if you want to stay. And I can't say I'd mind you hanging around, knowing that you're keeping an eye on things that could go boom."

"Sure thing. Can't say I've ever been given the VIP status before, so it'll be a nice change."

Candace cleared her throat. "Ah, do you have a partner or anyone I should add to the list, too?"

"Yeah, but he's probably not that interested in a show."

"Oh." He was gay? She sure hadn't seen that one coming, and it wasn't exactly easy to hide her disappointment. "If you're sure, then."

Logan met her gaze, his eyes dancing with what appeared to be...humor? "You've already met him, actually."

She swallowed, trying to figure out why he looked like he was about to burst into laughter again. "I have?"

"Yep. He's pretty big, beautiful brown eyes...and he's staring at you right now."

It took her half a second before she locked eyes with the dog staring at her, his black tail thumping against the ground as she showed him a hint of attention, like he'd figured the joke out before she had.

"That wasn't funny," she said, shaking her head and refusing to smile.

"Sorry, couldn't help myself."

"So, just the one pass, then?" she asked.

"Just the one," he confirmed, standing up when a knock at the door echoed throughout the room.

Candace watched as Logan accepted the food and kicked the door shut behind him. He wasn't hard to watch, the kind of guy she'd always notice no matter where she met him—tall, built and with close-cropped dark hair that matched his eyes. But he was strictly off-limits, eye candy only, because she was staying true to her promise not to get involved with anyone at the moment.

He paused, stood there looking down at her before crossing the room again.

"Candace, I won't be offended if you say no, but are you busy after your show?"

Why did he want to know, and why did he suddenly look so...staunch? "Why's that?"

Logan cleared his throat "I thought you might like a night out in Sydney, you know, to just have fun once you're done with work." He laughed. "I've been working around the clock for months, and I have a feeling you don't take much time off, either."

Candace stared at him, taken aback. He'd just managed to surprise her twice in less than a few minutes. "It's not that I don't want to, but it's just not that easy for me to hang out in public." Was he asking her on a date or did he think taking her out was part of his job description?

He put the containers down on the low table between the two sofas and sat down, leaning forward, eyes on hers. "You're in Australia, not America, and the places I'll take you, if it's just the two of us, no one will even realize who you are." Logan held his hands up. "But I have thick skin, so you can just turn me down and I'll forget I ever asked."

She took the plastic tops off the containers and reached for a pair of chopsticks, before looking up and seeing the serious expression on Logan's face. He was serious. And she had no idea what to say to him.

"You promise I'd be safe? That it would just be the two of us?"

"I promise," he said. "You'll just be a girl in the crowd instead of a superstar."

A shiver cascaded down her spine, spreading warmth into her belly. *Now that was something she liked the sound of.* "I'll think about it, but it does sound nice." It sounded way better than nice, but she didn't want to lead him on, not until she'd had time to think about it.

"Well, you just let me know when you're good and ready," he said. "Now it's time for you to tell me exactly what I'm about to bite into here, because I haven't ever seen anything that looks like this before."

Candace didn't usually even talk much before a show, tried to rest her voice, yet here she was chatting with a cute guy and thinking about going out with him. Maybe Australia was exactly the place she was supposed to be right now, to take her mind off everything that had been troubling her since…way too long.

* * *

Logan fought not to grimace as he held the chopsticks—awkwardly. He wasn't opposed to trying new things, but the food sitting in front of him looked downright scary. Not to mention the fact that he was more comfortable using a good old knife and fork.

"When you said Japanese, I was kind of thinking about the over-processed chicken sushi that I find at the mall."

Candace gave him her wide smile again, the one that was making him wish he'd met her under different circumstances. Although, someone like her wouldn't exactly have crossed paths with him if he hadn't been assigned to mind her. She was an international superstar and he was…a soldier turned bodyguard for a couple of days. Which was why he'd taken his chance to ask her out while he could. That would teach his friends for pestering him about being single too long and not enjoying enough human company—he'd stepped completely outside of his comfort level with Candace.

"So, I probably should have explained to you that sashimi is raw fish, huh?"

Logan raised his eyebrows and wrangled with the chopsticks some more, trying to mimic her actions. Except she was already dunking her first piece in the soy sauce and popping the entire thing in her mouth, which meant she was way ahead of him.

"Here goes," he muttered, leaning over the table so he didn't spill any, his other hand ready to catch anything that fell.

"What do you think?" she asked.

He swallowed. "I can't say I've ever wanted to eat raw fish before, but I guess it's not half bad."

"I do have one kind with a cooked prawn on top. Here," Candace said, opening another box and then pushing it his way. "Try this."

Logan shook his head. "I can't go eating your favorite foods hours before your big concert. I'm the help, not a guest."

She rolled her eyes. "If we eat all this I can order more, so just take whatever you like, okay?"

Logan stared at her, wondering if he was about to see her diva side firsthand. He had a feeling someone that beautiful and talented was bound to be difficult. "You're sure?"

"Look, most celebrities have a rider about exactly what they do and don't want backstage or in their dressing room. Me? I just ask to have someone ready to run out and grab me great Japanese food and bottled water, and I request good lighting for my hair and makeup team." She smiled, shrugging at the same time. "I like the fact that everyone thinks I'm easy to deal with, so trust me when I say we can order more. These people are used to divas requesting a certain number of candles with a particular scent, flowers, bowls filled with expensive chocolates and imported candy. You get my drift?"

Logan got the picture. "Okay, pass me the prawn one, then."

"That's more like it."

Candace pushed the container closer to him, as well as a cup with a lid on it.

"What's this?"

"Miso soup. You'll love it."

Logan took off the lid, staring into the brownish liquid. "You sure this stuff won't kill me?"

"Positive. Now stir it with your chopsticks and take a sip. The green stuff is just seaweed, and there might be a few pieces of tofu floating around, too."

"Tofu?" he asked, pausing before the cup touched his lips. "You're killing me. I don't even think Ranger would eat tofu."

As if he understood exactly what they were saying, Ranger let out a low whine that made Candace laugh.

"Tofu," Logan muttered, taking a sip.

It wasn't half as bad as he was expecting, so he had some more, careful to avoid anything solid that was floating around in the soup. He was probably the only person in the building who hadn't tried this type of food before, but he was a soldier and a rancher—he was more used to simple steaks, vegetables and fries than the latest cuisines. Not to mention he was having to act like a regular guy instead of one who usually couldn't go a day without exercising like a crazy thing—sprinting as hard as he could to outrun his demons.

"So, what do you think?" Candace asked, pulling her long hair from her face and throwing it back over her shoulders.

"I think," he said, clearing his throat and putting down his chopsticks, "that it's time I went and did another perimeter check."

He was starting to become way too comfortable sitting around with Candace, eating fancy food like he did it every day.

Smoke billowed around him, obscuring almost everything. He walked slowly, not able to see even one of his feet, but he never let go of Ranger's leash. And then he stumbled, looked down and realized he'd just walked over another human being, facedown in the sand.

Logan cleared his throat, pushing away the memories that always hit him when he was least expecting them. If he wasn't on duty, he would have changed his shoes and hit the gym. But today that wasn't an option, and neither was giving in to his memories.

CHAPTER TWO

CANDACE TOOK A deep breath, mentally preparing for the concert. She'd been given her sixty-minute countdown already, which meant it was time to start running through her exercises, have a little something to drink, stretching out so she was all limbered up and dressing in her first costume.

But preparing for the performance wasn't taking up all her energy like it should have been. Instead she was thinking about a certain man who'd as good as knocked the wind from her earlier in the afternoon.

She'd been single for so long, not to mention the fact that she hadn't met a man who'd even remotely interested her for close to a year. Maybe that was why Logan had surprised her so much. Because even if she stayed true to her promise to remain single, she could still appreciate a good-looking man. And Logan was a fine-looking addition to the male species.

Candace cleared her throat and was about to start rehearsing when there was a knock at the door. She didn't call out because she was saving her voice, but she did cross the room to see who it was.

"Hey."

The man she'd been trying her best not to think about was standing in the hallway.

"How did you get past my security detail?" she asked in a low voice.

Logan grinned. "It just so happens I know the boss."

She laughed and pulled open the door so he could come in. She was about to ask him in when he held his hand up and shook his head.

"I'm not going to disturb you, I just wanted to check that you felt safe," he told her. "I personally handpicked the men working tonight, so you've got nothing to worry about, and I'm going off duty now for a quick break."

Candace thought for a second before saying what was on her mind. "What do you think about escorting me to stage and watching from the wings?"

"Like my own private concert?" he asked, raising an eyebrow.

She grinned. The idea of having Logan close by in case something *did* happen would be reassuring.

"What if I made you a trade?" she asked.

He cocked his head, clearly listening.

"I'll say yes to the night out you suggested, tonight, if you look after me for the duration of my performance."

Logan didn't even blink he answered her so fast. "You're on."

Candace met Logan's gaze, determined to keep her head held high. He was a handsome man who happened to be protecting her, and one she'd agreed to go on a date of sorts with. It didn't mean she had to go all bashful and forget the confident woman she usually was.

"Well, that's settled then," she said. "I'm going to keep running through my routine, so if you could come back in about forty-five minutes?"

Logan nodded. "Yes, ma'am."

Candace forced herself to stop staring at the tall, heavily muscled hunk standing outside her door and shut it instead, slowly slithering to the floor once she did so, cool timber against her back. She was behaving like a silly girl, flirting with a man who probably had no interest in her other than to parade her around a few hotspots on his arm. How many times before had she had someone say to her that they wanted to take her on a quiet date, only to find the paparazzi tipped off the moment they arrived at a restaurant or club? Or a man pretending he wasn't interested in her fame, only to find out he was a wannabe film star or singer with a CD he wanted to slip her during drinks or over an entrée. *That* was why she'd sworn off men for the time being.

Deep down, she wanted to believe that Logan was different, but until he'd proven that he wasn't the type of guy she was used to, she needed to tread lightly. No falling for her bodyguard, no touching her bodyguard and definitely no letting herself think, at any stage, that he could be anything more than fun.

She'd tried serious, and it hadn't worked. She'd even tried marriage, too, and that hadn't worked out well at all. When it came to men, she'd realized that maybe she just wasn't good at picking them, and it was probably something she'd inherited from her mom. Her mom might have been an incredible businesswoman, but she'd also had to raise Candace singlehandedly because of her poor decisions when it came to the male species.

Candace sighed, reached out for her first outfit, ran her hands down the silk, shut her eyes and imagined herself on stage, wearing it. Listening to the crowd. Holding the microphone as the band started to play. Hair and makeup would be back any minute, and so would her stylist.

She could do this. She'd performed a hundred times before, and Logan had promised her that the venue was safe and secure. She needed to forget the stupid threats and just do what she did best. Because no matter what happened to her, no one could ever take away her love of singing. Performing was the love of her life and it always would be.

This was her time to shine.

"You a fan of country music?"

Logan glanced at the woman standing beside him, her headset pulled back so she could talk to him. She was holding a tablet, and until now she'd had her eyes glued to it and had been speaking intently into her headset.

"I can't say I've ever really listened to it before," he admitted. Truth be told, he'd never listened to it because he'd never really liked it before, but watching this particular performance was fast converting him to the genre.

"She's pretty incredible to watch," the woman said, pulling on her headset again. "I get to see a lot of performers, but she's hands down the most talented and nicest we've hosted yet."

Logan smiled in reply and turned his attention back to Candace. As the song finished she wowed the crowd with her mesmerizing, soft laugh, before turning around and waving toward the band so they could have their own round of applause. He was pleased that she'd asked him to watch, but he'd actually been employed to stay until the end of her concert anyway. He just hadn't told her that.

"Thank you for having me here tonight!" she told her fans. "Australia is one of the most beautiful countries I've ever visited, and I wish I had more time to spend here."

The applause was deafening, but Logan could no more take his eyes off her and walk away than he could stop breathing. If there was such a thing as star power, she had it—on stage she wasn't the sweet, soft-spoken woman he'd spent time with earlier in the day. Up there, her presence was almost overpowering, and the screaming fans only seemed to make her light up more in front of them, her confidence soaring as they encouraged her.

As she burst into another song, Logan leaned against the wall where he was standing. The past year had been nothing short of hard, unbearable, and being here tonight, watching Candace, was the kind of night he'd needed, even if it was technically work.

When Sam had died...*hell.* He didn't want to go back there. Losing one of his closest friends so soon after his parents' accident, then coming so close to losing another under different circumstances, not to mention deciding to retire—he'd only just pulled through. But the rush he'd felt when Candace had said yes to a night out with him had given him a much needed boost. He was ready to add some nice memories to his thought bank, and Candace was exactly the kind of memory he'd prefer to dwell upon.

He looked up as the next song came to an end, and the next thing he knew Candace was running toward him.

"What did you think?" she asked, eyes flashing as she glanced at him, a big smile on her face as she ran in her heels. "The crowd is crazy here!"

She kept moving, not pausing, so Logan spun and jogged to keep up with her, even as she was surrounded by a group of people who started to tug at her clothes and talk a million miles an hour.

"You were great out there," he managed when the crowd paused for a nanosecond.

"You really think so?"

There was an innocence in her gaze that made Logan smile, because this was the woman he'd glimpsed earlier. The one who was so used to being told by others what they thought she wanted to hear, that she no longer knew who to believe, who to trust. She wanted to know whether she could believe him—it was so obvious it was written all over her face, and he had no more intention of lying to her than anyone else.

"I know so," he told her honestly.

The words were barely out of his mouth before she disappeared into her dressing room, and Logan turned his back when he realized the door wasn't going to be closed. It seemed like only minutes later that she was running back out again, heading toward the stage, and instead of trying to keep up with her this time he just walked behind. She was still being plucked and prodded, her outfit pulled into shape and her hair fiddled with just before she was due back on stage. The woman with the tablet from earlier was flapping her arms at a group of dancers, before starting a countdown and sending them on as the music started again.

Just before she disappeared, Candace turned and locked her gaze on his, smiling for barely a second before throwing one hand in the air and returning to the stage.

There was no doubting she was a brilliant performer, but she was also like a little girl desperately in need of someone to look after her and trust in. To tell her the truth when she needed it, but also to shield her from harm.

"I'm not that person," Logan muttered to himself, even as his instinct to protect reared within him before he could stamp it out.

He'd protected and looked after people all his life, and still he'd lost those he loved. Some of the people he cared most about in the world, and some strangers whose faces he'd never forget until the day he died, too. Looking after Candace while she was on stage and during her press conference tomorrow was his job, and one he intended on doing well, and tonight was about having fun with a beautiful woman. There was no need to overthink the situation or turn it into something it wasn't.

He wasn't going to be the one to rescue her, because

he was still waiting to be rescued himself. Tonight was going to be great, but after that he'd never see her again, which meant she wasn't his to worry about. Or protect.

Candace took one last bow after her second encore song before walking from the stage. It had been the kind of night she loved, the type that made her remember how lucky she was to perform for a career, even though her nerves had jangled whenever she'd let her mind stray to the hate mail she'd been receiving. There were always those times when she wondered if that person was in the crowd, watching her, but with Logan standing in the wings and the security amped up for the evening, she'd tried to make herself just relax. And for the most part it had worked.

Her heart was still pounding, adrenaline making her feel a million dollars, as she disappeared into the darkness of the wings, her eyes taking a moment to adjust from the bright lights she'd been performing under.

"I think you've made me like country music," a deep male voice said.

She recognized Logan's Australian twang the moment she heard it, and her heart started to race a little more.

"I'd say I don't believe you, but I kind of want to," she said with a laugh.

"I'm actually thinking of joining your insane fans and lining up for a CD and T-shirt. It seems to be the thing to do."

She laughed, brushing her hand against his as she passed and then snatching it back like she'd connected with a flame. It had been a long time since she'd just touched someone impulsively like that, and it wasn't something she wanted to make a habit of. Especially not with a man, even if she was enjoying his company.

"You can have a free T-shirt, I'll even autograph it for you," she teased.

"So what time do you want to head out?" he asked, following her.

Candace took a slow breath, still energized from her ninety minutes on stage. She always felt amazing at the end of a performance, exhaustion never setting in for hours after she finished.

"We'll need to wait until the crowds die down. I don't mind signing a couple of autographs, but I'm not going to ruin my buzz by being mobbed. Not tonight."

Logan shook his head. "I think we're best to leave immediately, before anyone expects you to depart. My truck's parked around the back and we should be able to get in before anyone realizes it's you, so long as we move quickly."

Candace wasn't convinced, but then she also usually timed these kind of things all wrong anyway and ended up in the middle of a hundred fans, trying to reach her getaway car. Or else her manager set things up to happen like that for maximum publicity when she gave him explicit instructions to the contrary.

"I don't believe you, but I'm prepared to give you the benefit of the doubt," she said.

"Good. I'll go check the exit now and be back in ten minutes," he told her. "Shall we meet in your dressing room?"

Candace nodded. "Let's do it."

The idea of a night out was exciting—she'd become used to feeling fantastic, on a high from singing, then going straight back to a hotel room, alone. Most of the time she ended up ordering room service, watching an old movie and going to bed, before receiving her wake-up call and taking a car to the airport early the next morning. Before she'd become recognizable, she'd always had a fun night out after any gig, which was why tonight was like a blast from the past for her. Add the tourism campaign she was the face of, and she didn't have a hope of Australians not realizing who she was.

It was yet to be seen whether she could even manage to leave the building without being recognized or followed, so she could easily end up holed up in her hotel room just when she least expected it.

Candace closed her dressing room door the moment she stepped inside and slipped the feathery minidress off, letting it pool to the floor. She rummaged around in her case for the casual clothes she'd packed, in case she needed them, pulling out a pair of dark blue skinny jeans and wriggling her way into them. She didn't have anything other than a T-shirt to wear, so she flicked through the tops hanging on her racks, wishing they weren't all so costume looking, until she spotted a sequined black tank. Candace pulled it over her head, grabbed a studded leather biker jacket, and slipped into a pair of dangerously high heels she'd worn on stage earlier in the evening.

Glancing at the clock on the wall, she stopped, took a deep breath, then sat down at her dressing table. Her

makeup was excessive—thick false eyelashes and spar-
kly eyeshadow—but she didn't have time to change it.
Besides, Logan had seen her looking like this all evening. She did run her fingers through her hair to flatten
it down a bit, teasing the hairspray from her curls so it
felt like real hair again, so it was touchable.

There was a knock at the door. Candace jumped,
glaring at her reflection at the same time. It was just
Logan, and it wasn't like she hadn't known he was coming, but her nerves had been permanently on edge for
weeks now. Maybe she could talk to him about it and see
what he thought the best way to react to the threats was.

"Just a minute!" she called out.

Candace jumped up to grab her purse, checked her
credit card, phone and hotel swipe card were all inside
and swung open the door.

"Wow."

Logan's approving smile and the way he looked her
up and down made her laugh. He seemed to say what
he was thinking, and she liked the fact he was a straight
shooter with her.

"Are we cleared to leave?" she asked, trying to ignore what he'd just said even though she couldn't stop
smiling.

"I told your manager and the rest of the team that
you're feeling ill, and you wanted me to escort you
straight to the hotel. I said we'll be exiting from the
side entrance, and I have a feeling there'll be a lot of
fans waiting there, if you catch my drift."

"So we can't go?" she asked, hearing the disappointment in her own voice.

Logan gave her a wry smile, a dimple flashing against his cheek at the same time. "We're going out the very back. My vehicle's parked down the alleyway, so no one will see us."

"So you lied to everyone?" she asked.

"I expanded the truth," he said, winking as he gestured for her to follow him. "I have a feeling your manager is more interested in getting publicity than a quiet getaway for you, and given that I'm your head of security, all I care about is your safety. You say no fans or paparazzi? That's what I give you."

Candace shook her head. "I think I underestimated you," she said with a chuckle.

"I also told them that you'd be exiting in fifteen minutes, so if we're going to do this, I think we should hurry, just in case someone comes looking for you before we go."

He waited for her to nod, then clasped her hand firmly, walking fast in the opposite direction to which they'd arrived earlier in the day. Candace had to almost run to keep up with his long, loping stride, but she didn't care. Logan was going to get her out of here without being mobbed, without even having to come face-to-face with her manager, and she might actually have a drink at a bar before anyone figured out who she was. Adrenaline was starting to fill her with hope.

Her phone started to beep in her purse, and she managed to open it without slowing down. She glanced at the screen.

"It's Billy, my manager," she told Logan when he looked down.

"Text him from the car when we're driving away," he said. "You can tell him we've gone once we've hit the main road, but not before."

Candace slipped the phone back into her purse and hurried along with Logan, trying to concentrate on not falling off her stiletto heels. A few little white lies weren't going to hurt anyone, especially not her manager, who didn't seem to care that she'd spent the past few weeks frightened out of her own skin about the thought of being in public.

"So did you believe me when I said I'd get you out of there?"

Logan glanced over at Candace and saw that she was staring out the window, watching the world as it blurred past.

"No," she replied, sighing and turning in her seat to face him. "If I'm completely honest I didn't even want to let myself hope that I'd get out of there that easily."

"So I don't need to ask you if you're still keen for a few drinks and something to eat?"

Candace laughed and it made him smile. "I'll stay out until someone starts flashing camera bulbs in my face."

"You're on. The places I'm taking you no one will ever find us."

She was looking out the window again, and he took his foot off the gas a little so they weren't going so fast. For someone who hadn't found it easy being back or dealing with people, he was finding it weirdly easy to talk to Candace. She should be the one person he had nothing in common with, but for some reason he was drawn to the fact that she was an outcast just like he was, albeit a different one. It settled him somehow.

"That kind of makes you sound like a serial killer," she finally responded, like she was just thinking out aloud. "Which makes me wonder how I ended up letting you whisk me away from everyone who's supposed to be looking after me and keeping me safe."

"I'm the one who kept you safe today, so you don't have a lot to worry about," Logan told her, taking his eyes off the road for a second to make sure she was listening to him, looking at him. "If I'm perfectly honest, you have a manager who makes sure you get mobbed when he knows you hate it, and the rest of your entourage probably have way less interest in making sure you're kept out of harm's way than I do."

She shut her eyes and put her head against the rest. "I know you're right about my manager. Deep down, I think I've known it for a while. I just didn't want to acknowledge it."

He didn't answer. He knew he was right, but he didn't need to make her feel worse than she probably already did.

"Until you said that, I guess I've been trying to bury my head in the sand and pretend like everything's fine."

Logan fought the battle to bite his tongue and lost. "The guy's seriously bad news. How long have you put up with him for? I know you have more experience with the whole celebrity thing than I ever will, but that's a layperson's take on him."

Candace sighed. "He's been with me for years, and

he used to be a lot better than he is now, that's for sure," she muttered. "Things have kind of been going down-hill for a while now."

"How about we stop talking about work and just have a nice night?" Logan suggested, wishing he'd just kept his mouth shut instead of insulting her people. For once in his life he wasn't screwing up—usually something he only managed to achieve in his work life—and he needed to just enjoy the company of a beautiful woman.

"You betcha," Candace agreed. "Hey, where's your dog tonight?"

Logan grimaced. "I left him at home. He was pretty pissed."

"You know, for a dog he's kind of nice."

"You're a cat person, aren't you?"

She laughed, like she was embarrassed. "Sure am. I was attacked by a German Shepherd when I was a little girl. In fact, I still have the scars to prove it. I've just never really warmed to dogs since. Stupid, I know, but just the way I am."

"Understandable." Personally, he wasn't fussed on cats, but he wasn't going to tell her that. "I've had dogs all my life, but then I've never had one be anything other than loyal to me."

"Back home I have a pair of Birman cats called Indie and Lexie, and if I'm completely honest they've prob-ably done me more damage with their claws than your dog has probably ever done to you with his teeth."

They both laughed. Logan changed the subject for a second, wanting to point out to Candace where they were going.

"See just over there? That's Cockle Bay and it's where I'm taking you for dinner."

"I thought we were just going for drinks?" she asked, her nose almost pressed to the window, looking where he'd pointed.

It was the reason Logan had brought her here, because he knew how amazing the harbor was to visitors. Him? He'd grown up with it and was used to it, but every time he'd returned from a tour it had always put a smile on his face, told him he was home.

"If you're not hungry, we can always skip dinner."

"Don't be silly. After all that energy I used on stage, I'm famished," she admitted. "And dinner sounds great."

Logan parked his four-by-four and jumped out, grabbing his jacket and pulling it on. He walked around the vehicle and opened the passenger door, waiting for Candace to step out.

"Thank you," she said. "You know, it's kind of strange for me getting out on this side of the road."

Logan waited for her to grab her purse, before shutting the door and leading the way, walking slowly so she didn't have to hurry beside him.

"Your shoes are insanely high."

"I know, but aren't they fab? They were a gift from my favorite designer."

He raised his eyebrows. "You're talking to a soldier, sorry. But they do look cool, I guess, for a pair of shoes, that is."

Candace laughed. "I definitely need to spend more

time with real people. Of course you couldn't care less about my shoes!"

He shrugged and pointed ahead. "We're going to a place called Jimmy's and they have the best seafood in Sydney. Plus they're right on the water."

Candace started walking even slower, a smile spreading over her face that he couldn't miss as they passed a couple who didn't even look at them.

"You have no idea what it feels like to just walk along the street and not be noticed. I've missed this for so long now."

Logan looked up, taking comfort in the bright stars twinkling in the dark sky—the same stars he'd looked at every night when he was on tour even though he'd been on the other side of the world. When he was at home in the Outback, they always seemed brighter, but they were still just as pretty to look at in the city.

"When I was on my first couple of tours, white soldiers were pretty easy to notice. I remember the first time we went through a village, and the women were screaming out to us, begging us to help them. I couldn't understand what they were saying, but the pleading, desperate looks they were giving us told me that I was their last chance. That that's how they thought of us." Logan took a deep breath, wondering why he was even telling Candace all this. He hardly ever spoke about his tours, except with Brett, but for some reason he just needed her to know. "These little children were hanging on to us, grabbing us as we walked through on patrol, and we gave them all the food we had. It wasn't until the next day that we found out all the men had been killed by local insurgents, and the women were left to fend on their own, terrified that they'd be next, and with no way to provide for their children."

Candace had almost stopped walking now, her eyes like saucers, filled with tears as she stared at him. Her hands were clenched into fists at her sides.

"What happened to them?"

Logan shook his head. "I don't know. But I can tell you how awful it was to be recognized, as someone who those people thought could save them, when in reality all I could offer was some dried snacks and a candy bar. And it happened to us over and over again."

"So, what you're saying is that I need to stop caring about being recognized for who I am?" she asked, her voice soft.

"No, what I'm saying is that sometimes being recognized for the right reasons is okay. The people who want to see you just want a smile and an autograph, and they're things you can give them. It's when you're powerless that being recognized is something to be scared of."

Candace shook her head, a sad look on her face. "I sound like a selfish, self-centered idiot for even saying all that, when you compare it to what you went through. But I guess it's just that I struggle with the whole fame thing. I'm a singer and I love what I do. It's just the publicity that I find really difficult." She sighed. "Unfortunately one doesn't come without the other in this industry."

"No, Candace, that's not what I meant," he said as they started to walk again. "I guess I just want you to know that I probably understand some of what you go through on a daily basis, even though our worlds are light-years apart."

They walked in silence for a minute, almost at the restaurant. She knew what he meant, but she still felt stupid for moaning aloud about being recognized. She was lucky and she knew it, but lately being surrounded by fans had turned from flattering to downright scary.

"Have you ever tried Morton Bay bugs?" Logan asked, changing the subject.

Candace gave him a look like she was trying to figure out if he was joking. "I have no idea what you're even talking about, but they sound revolting."

He laughed. "Definitely not revolting, I promise you. They're kind of like lobster, but different. Better."

"You're serious, aren't you?" she groaned as he opened the door. "You're actually going to make me eat something called a *bug as punishment for the sashimi.*"

"It's a stupid name for what they are, but yeah, you're definitely going to be eating them." Logan chuckled as they stood and waited to be greeted. "Grilled with garlic butter, fresh bread on the side and…"

"Logan?"

He spun around, taking his eyes off Candace and her cute smile. "Hey, Jimmy."

His old friend raised his eyebrows, looking from him to Candace, before his eyes widened. Logan gave him a look that he hoped he understood, not wanting their night ruined before it even started.

"The kitchen's closing soon, but I can squeeze you two in if you order quick," Jimmy said, grabbing two menus. "How you been, anyway? I haven't seen you in ages."

Logan motioned for Candace to follow, touching his hand to her lower back and guiding her forward.

"I've been okay, can't complain. Especially since I'm back for good now."

Jimmy walked them through the restaurant and waved toward an alfresco table, complete with low candles on the table and a view out over the water. Even though it was dark, the water was twinkling under the lights from all the restaurants and the luxury yachts moored nearby. The night air was warm, slightly muggy still after the hot day.

"Do you even need these?" Jimmy asked with a grin, gesturing at the menus.

Logan grinned straight back at him, pulling out a seat for Candace. Jimmy obviously knew exactly who she was—maybe he was just too starstruck to remember his manners, or his job.

"Let's start with two buckets of prawns and sourdough bread, then Morton Bay bugs for two, and maybe a Caesar salad."

Jimmy was nodding, but he was also spending most of his time glancing at Candace, who was looking out at the water, her body turned away from them.

Logan leaned in closer to his childhood friend, giving him a playful whack across the back of the head.

"Don't you breathe a word of this to anyone until we're gone. No tipping the media off, no telling your girlfriend."

Jimmy made a face like his head hurt, but he was

still grinning. "Can I at least get an autograph before you leave?"

"Keep everyone else away from us and I'll make sure you get one. Deal?"

Jimmy's smile grew wider. "And a big tip, too, right?"

"You do know I have a dog that could eat you in a few mouthfuls, don't you?" Logan said in a low voice, smiling as Candace turned to face them.

Jimmy just laughed. "I'll get your order in and bring you some drinks. Champagne?"

Logan sat down and glanced at Candace. "Bubbly or beer?"

She made a thoughtful face before one side of her mouth tilted up into a smile. "Let's have a beer. Why not?"

Logan didn't let the surprise show on his face, even though he'd never have picked her choosing beer over champagne in a million years. "You heard the lady. Two beers, bottles not glasses."

Jimmy shook his head and walked off, leaving Logan to burst out laughing. Candace seemed to be finding the entire thing as hilarious as he was.

"He knew who I was the moment we walked in, didn't he?" she asked in a soft voice, like she wasn't in the least bit surprised.

Logan wasn't going to lie to her. "Yeah, he did. But there's no way he's going to make a fuss or say anything, okay?"

She nodded. "So you don't think it'll be in the papers that I was spotted out with a mystery man, knocking back beers? Knowing the paps, they'll probably say I was out of control and ready for rehab."

"You missed the part about us digging into two massive buckets filled with prawns, that we'll be eating with our fingers like barbarians instead of fine dining."

Candace dipped her head when she laughed, looking up at him like she wasn't entirely sure whether he was ever being serious or always joking. "And here I was thinking you'd brought me to a classy restaurant."

"Believe me, nothing in the world is better than fresh seafood eaten with your fingers, washed down by an ice-cold beer. We don't need five forks and silver service to eat incredible food."

"Well, I'll have to reserve judgment until I've experienced it, but I'm guessing you're probably right."

He leaned back in his chair. "See the beautiful super yachts out there?"

She nodded, following his gaze.

"When you come here earlier in the evening, there are waiters running back and forth from the restaurant to the boats, carrying silver trays of seafood and champagne. It's crazy, but a lot of fun to watch."

"I was right going with my gut feeling on promoting Australia to the world," she said with a laugh. "Next time I'm ready for a vacation, I'm heading straight back here."

CHAPTER THREE

CANDACE LOOKED BACK out at the water to avoid looking at the man seated across from her. There was something exciting about being out somewhere different, on the other side of the world, and with someone she hardly knew. And for the first time in forever, she actually felt like herself, like the old her, the one she'd started to slowly lose a few years earlier. When her marriage had started to crumble, so had her self-confidence, and then when her mom had died…she pushed the dark thoughts away and focused on Logan.

"Is this somewhere you come often?"

Logan leaned forward, both hands on his beer bottle. She took a sip of hers while she waited for his response.

"I've been coming here for years. Every time I came home from deployment, this was the first place I headed to for a meal," he told her. "There were three of us with a standing date."

"As in three soldiers?" she asked, curious.

Logan twirled his beer bottle between his hands. "Yeah."

Candace could sense there was something else going

on, something unsaid, but she didn't know him well enough to pry. She knew what it was like to want to keep some things private.

"It must have been a relief coming here for the amazing food after what you had to eat over there," she said, wanting to give him an out if he needed it.

Logan looked up and met her gaze. "It was. There's only so much dried jerky and dehydrated food a guy can eat, right?"

She laughed, but it died in her throat as their waiter approached the table with an enormous amount of food.

"No way."

Logan grinned and leaned back as two large silver buckets filled with prawns were placed in front of them. She'd never seen so much seafood in her life.

"You're telling me that this is just for starters?" she asked, groaning.

The waiter returned with two dishes of some kind of sauce and freshly quartered lemons, as well as a bowl of warm water, which she guessed was for them to dip their fingers in to after eating.

"In Australia, we have a saying that you can't eat enough seafood," Logan told her.

"You do?" Candace watched as he picked up one of the prawns and pulled the head off, before peeling the shell.

"No, I just made that up to make you think this was a good idea." He gave her a wink that made her heart thud to her toes. "If you don't want to get your hands dirty I can peel yours?" he offered.

"I appreciate the gesture but I think it's about time

I got my hands dirty." She was sick of people running around and doing everything for her, and tonight was about her just being her. "You show me what to do and I'll do it."

"You just have to grab your beer bottle between your palms so it doesn't get all greasy. Like this," Logan explained, demonstrating with a quick swig of his beer before dipping his prawn into the sauce.

Candace just shook her head, finding it hard to believe that she'd been performing live in front of twenty thousand people only an hour earlier, and was now sitting at a restaurant, tucking into a meal with the man who'd been assigned her personal head of security. Add to that the fact she hadn't been asked for even one autograph…it was insane. She shouldn't have trusted him so easily, but she hadn't been so relaxed in a long time. Maybe she'd wake up and realize it had all just been a dream, but if it had been, at least it had been a nice one.

She peeled her first prawn and dipped it in the sauce.

"Good?" he asked.

"Amazing," she murmured, hand over her mouth as she spoke. "You were right."

They sat in silence for a while, both eating their prawns and sipping beer. Something told her that Logan wasn't usually a big talker—that he was comfortable not saying anything at all, and she liked it. Where she'd grown up, the men had a motto of speaking only when they'd had something worthy of being said, but her adult life had been filled with men who couldn't say *enough* to make themselves sound important.

"So have you always lived in the city?" she asked.

Logan looked up, finishing his mouthful and dipping his fingers in the lemon water to clean them. She watched as he dried his hands on the napkin.

"I actually grew up in the Outback," he told her, finishing his beer before leaning back in his chair. "I'm based here a lot of the time, but when I'm not working I head straight back there just to be away from the city and out in the open air."

So, that's why she felt so comfortable around him. It had been a while since she'd hung out with a country boy.

"Your family all ranch out there?"

He grinned. "We call it farming here, but yeah, it's my family property."

Candace paused, slowly peeling a prawn. "So your dad runs the place or a brother?"

Logan took a deep breath, she could see the rise and fall of his chest, before he waved to a waiter and gestured for another beer. He glanced at her, but Candace shook her head—hers was still half-full.

He cleared his throat. "My parents both died a few years ago, and my sister lives on a farm with her husband," Logan explained. "The property has been in our family for generations, so I'd rather die than sell the place, but I've had to have a manager employed while I've been serving so the place can continue to run smoothly."

Candace sighed. "I shouldn't have been so nosey, Logan. I'm sorry."

"It's fine. Sometimes it's just hard to say out loud,

because admitting it makes it real, as stupid as that sounds."

She knew exactly how that felt. "My mom died a couple of years ago, and if I'm honest, that's why I've put up with my management team for longer than I should have. She was the one who dealt with all that stuff so I could just focus on singing, and I'm still pretty lost without her. She was the business brains and I was the creative one, and it had always been just the two of us. We made a good team."

Logan took the beer that arrived at their table, his eyes leaving hers to look out at the water. She did the same, because it seemed wrong to keep watching him when he was obviously troubled about what they were talking about. He was silent.

"I didn't mean to just unleash all that on you," she apologized. "I don't usually spill my thoughts so easily, but…"

"It's nice to tell someone who actually gets it, right?" he finished, gaze meeting hers again.

"Yeah," she murmured, "something like that."

"Losing a parent is tough, and it doesn't get easier, so don't believe anyone if they try to tell you otherwise," he told her. "But you do learn to live with it."

Their table was cleared then and within minutes two large white plates were placed in front of them.

"So these are the bugs, huh?"

Logan nodded, but he was more reserved now than he'd been before—his enthusiasm dulled.

"You just scoop the white meat out of the shell," he told her. "It's incredible."

Candace spread her napkin over her lap, smoothing out the wrinkles, before picking up her fork and following Logan's lead. He was right—again—the food was great.

"Thanks for a lovely evening," she told him when she'd finished her mouthful. "It was completely unexpected and I appreciate the gesture."

He gave her a weird look. "Sounds like you're ready to leave."

"No, I'm just grateful that I've actually enjoyed a night in someone else's company. You've given me some perspective at a time when I needed it."

Logan went back to getting every last piece of meat from the shellfish, and she forced herself to stop watching him and just eat, too. There was something so refreshingly real about him.

"Another beer?"

She looked at her bottle and was about to say no, before she changed her mind. "You know what? Yeah. I'd love another. Why not?"

"So, I told you where I grew up. How about you?"

"I grew up on a ranch, too. My parents split when I was a baby, so we moved to my grandparents' ranch. I used to ride my horse and sing into a hairbrush, pretending it was my microphone. I spent every day outside, even if it was raining, just making up songs and enjoying the fresh air." She smiled just thinking about it. "It was the best childhood I could imagine, and my grandfather made up for my not having a dad. He was great."

He chuckled. "Ever wish you could go back in time?"

"I don't know about back in time, but I'd love to go

back to living on a ranch. I have a place in Montana, but it's not somewhere I get to very often these days, so it's not really where I call home."

"Why don't you just make time?"

Logan's question was serious, his voice deep.

"That's a very good question."

"Candace, when do you fly out?" Logan asked.

She pushed her plate away and reached for her beer. "Day after tomorrow."

Logan pulled a bread roll apart and took a bite, looking back out at the water again. There was a lot going on his mind, she was sure of it, but it was like he chose his words carefully, thought everything through before he said it. Their Caesar salad arrived while they were mid conversation, but there was no way she was going to able to eat even a mouthful of it.

"Why?"

"I was just thinking that spending some more time in Australia would do you the world of good."

"Meaning that I need to unwind?"

His eyes were still on the water, looking into the distance. "Meaning that if you want to remember what it's like to just be a human being in the world, here's probably the place to do it. The Outback heals the soul, or at least that's what I've always believed."

"Is that what the Outback did for you?" she asked, studying his side profile, the angle of his jaw and the fullness of his lips.

She glanced away when he turned, catching her staring.

"Yeah, it did," he said. "The Outback saved me when

nothing else could, and every time I go back there it reminds me what life is truly about. I guess it's my place in the world."

Candace didn't know why, or how, but when she saw the hurt in his gaze, the honesty of what he was saying, tears sprang into her eyes. This man who'd been so kind to her, so polite and respectful, had a power of hurt inside of him, and even glimpsing it made her sad. Whatever he'd been through was more than just losing his parents—he'd seen pain, grief, like she'd probably never know. What he'd experienced as a soldier must have given him memories that he'd never be able to shed.

"Excuse me, I'm just going to find the ladies' room," Candace said, grabbing her purse, before crossing the restaurant.

A waiter pointed her in the right direction and she disappeared into the first restroom, locking the door behind her. Candace stared at her reflection in the mirror, studying her face, seeing the makeup, the woman she was on stage, and not the girl she felt like inside.

The past few months, she'd been miserable except for the few times she'd been on stage or in the studio. So unhappy that she'd clung to what felt safe, what she thought was right, but one evening in the company of someone like Logan and she was starting to question everything. Today had been full of adrenaline and anticipation, she'd been excited when she'd said yes to going out with Logan, and now she was starting to spiral down, like a party girl coming off a high.

Logan was kind and handsome, and in all honesty she was probably drawn to him because he was capable of protecting her. But in less than two days she'd be flying away from Australia and never coming back, which was why she should never have agreed to tonight. Men were supposed to be off her radar, and after everything she'd been through, that's where she wanted them to stay. So getting her hopes up about an Australian soldier who'd probably never even think about her again, who probably just wanted what every other guy wanted from her, was beyond stupid.

Candace reapplied her lip gloss and gave herself a long, hard stare in the mirror. The best thing she could do was call it a night, not get involved in any way with Logan. For her sake and for his. She'd been stupid to agree to it in the first place.

Logan stood when Candace reappeared. He knew he was frowning, but the look on her face wasn't helping him to stop.

"You okay?" he asked.

"I'm fine," she replied, but he could tell from the smile she fixed that it was a face she'd perfected to hide how she really felt. He'd spent most of his working life studying people and situations, and he doubted he was wrong.

"Are you ready to head somewhere else for a drink, or..." He paused, watching the way her gaze darted away, the change in her eyes. "You're ready to go back to your hotel, aren't you?"

Candace nodded. "I think maybe we should call it a night."

Logan hesitated before reaching for her hand, not sure what he'd done to upset her.

"Candace, if there's something I've done..." he started.

"No, it's absolutely nothing you've done," she whispered, but as she spoke tears glinted in her eyes.

"It's been a long time since I've made a girl cry," he said, doing the only thing he could think of and pulling her toward him for a hug. "Whatever it is, I'm sorry."

She hardly moved, but her hand did reach up and grasp his shirt as he put his arms around her, held her so she could compose herself.

"I don't know why you're being so kind to me," she murmured, just loud enough for him to hear.

Logan sighed, inhaling the fresh scent of her hair, the aroma of her perfume. It had been a while since he'd been with a woman, and being this close to Candace was something he was already starting to crave.

"You sure you don't want another drink? Something else to eat?"

She ran her hand down his arm as she stepped back, eyes fixed on his. Logan was watching her, waiting for her to reply, when a flash went off, followed by what seemed like a hundred more. Logan leaped in front of Candace, instinct warning him to protect her no matter what, anger burning inside him as he realized the threat was only a photographer who'd managed to find them.

"Crap," he muttered, taking her hand firmly in his.

"It's okay, it's just one pap," she said.

He didn't care if it was one or twenty, he was still pissed at the intrusion. The photographer was escorted from the restaurant within minutes, but Logan knew it had been enough to rattle Candace. He had his own personal reasons to hate the media, and he wasn't going to let them ruin Candace's evening, not when she'd been so excited about an anonymous night out.

"Word will be out soon, so I'll take you straight to the hotel," he told her, before remembering what he'd promised Jimmy. "Before we go, I did promise our waiter an autograph in exchange for his discretion. If he was the one who tipped that guy off, I'll kill him, but I think I made it clear enough already what the consequences would be, so I doubt it would have been him."

Candace's smile diffused his anger as easily as someone blowing out a candle.

"Logan, we've sat here alone without anyone bothering us for the best part of a couple of hours. I don't care about one photographer finding us, but you're right about word not taking long to spread."

"So you're not angry?" He was confused—and he was seriously pissed.

Candace plucked a pen from her purse and signed an unused white napkin on their table.

"This is for your friend," she told him. "Do you want me to settle the bill and give it to him?"

Logan was reaching for the napkin when he froze. Had he just heard that right?

"You're not paying the bill."

"Of course I am," she said. "I wouldn't have it any other way."

"I asked you out for dinner, and I don't care how PC

the world is supposed to be, but you taking care of the bill is ridiculous."

"Logan—" she started, but he cut her off.

"Do you really want to insult me?" he asked.

"I'm just used to…"

"Jerks, if they let you pay. I don't care who you are. The only thing I care about is that you're a woman and I'm a man, and that means I take care of our bill tonight."

He watched as she shut her mouth and shrugged, clearly giving in. "Well, all right then. Thank you for a lovely meal, Mr. Neanderthal."

Logan burst out laughing as they walked to the front of the restaurant. "I know I'm old-fashioned, but seriously. Just because you're famous doesn't mean you shouldn't be treated like a lady."

He paid and passed his friend the napkin as they said goodbye, before walking out the front door.

"And just because you're a soldier doesn't mean you have to…"

Her words faded as someone yelled her name, and Logan sprung straight into work mode, putting his arm around her shoulders and hurrying her forward. There were a couple of guys trying to get close with their cameras, but he ignored them and just focused on propelling Candace away.

"We'll be fine once we get to the car," he told her, his palm firm on her shoulder.

"They'll follow us straight to my hotel."

"You want to go somewhere no one can bother you?" he asked.

"Please."

"Then I'll give them the slip and we can head straight to my place. No one will ever find you there."

Logan didn't know why he said it, why he'd even thought to take her back to his house, but he had and now there was no going back. The last time he'd let a woman into his home had been...Logan swallowed and moved faster, listening to Candace's heels as they beat a rhythm against the sidewalk. When he'd admitted to his friends that it had been a long time since he'd let a woman into his life, he hadn't been exaggerating.

He'd enjoyed tonight because he hadn't let himself dwell on the past, and if he wanted to survive having Candace at his place, then that's what he'd have to keep doing. There was no point thinking about the woman who'd hurt him, or anything else about what had happened in the past few years.

For months, he'd been telling himself that it was time to move on with his life, to put his past behind him, but some things were easy to think and a whole lot harder to put into practice. Especially when the darkness of his memories crept into his brain just when he was least expecting them.

CHAPTER FOUR

CANDACE COULD FEEL her heart racing—it was like her pulse was thumping in her head it sounded so loud. Fleeing the paparazzi and heading for Logan's place had seemed like the safe option when he'd suggested it, but now she was starting to panic. It was one thing to have dinner with the man in a public place, but going back to his house? Not something she'd ever usually do, especially with someone she'd just met, without anyone else knowing where she was.

They pulled up in front of a row of two-story houses. There wasn't a garage, so Logan parked on the street, and she waited for him to come around to open her door. It gave her time to calm her breathing and think about how to handle the situation.

"We managed to lose all of them, and I doubt they'll come looking for you in the suburbs."

She stepped out of the vehicle and shut the door behind her, before following Logan to the front door of his house. Nerves made her stomach flutter, but she ignored them. It was time she started trusting her own instincts.

"I should probably call my manager, just to let him

know where I am." Candace didn't like the fact that no one in the world knew where to find her if they needed her. Although come to think of it, she did have a tracking device on her phone, so her manager could locate her if he made an effort.

"Candace, you can do whatever you like, but if it were me? I'd be telling him you were safe and that you'd see him tomorrow. Unless you're okay with that same shark frenzy we just escaped from turning up outside here with telescopic lenses."

She grimaced. "You really don't like him, do you?"

"If I'm completely honest with you, I have my suspicions that the hate mail and threats you've been receiving aren't real. I don't want to point fingers, but there's only one person I can see who could be responsible, if my theory is correct."

Candace was sick to her stomach hearing his words, but she also realized that Logan could be right. She'd never have thought it before, *had never thought it,* but she also wasn't prepared to defend Billy without looking into it further. Without her mom to guide her, she knew she could have overlooked *something,* but if Logan's hunch was correct…She swallowed but refused to push the thoughts away like she usually would. She had only herself to rely on now, and that meant investigating the situation thoroughly if she needed to.

"Say you're right," she said. "What do you think I should do about it?"

"Ask him outright. I bet you'll figure it out the moment you catch him off guard and see the look on his face. Just trust your instincts, because they don't often let you down when you listen to them."

It was a serious accusation to make, but she would do exactly what Logan had suggested. What did she have to lose if she was wrong?

Logan flicked the lights on as he walked inside and she jumped back as his dog came bounding toward them.

"Hey, boy, settle down," he instructed, bending to give his dog some attention. "You remember Candace?"

She stayed in place, back to the front door, not certain about the excited canine. He was sitting to attention, perfectly obedient, but she still wasn't ready to trust him quite yet.

"Look, I just know Billy's type, and I'm a pretty good judge of people," Logan said, which made her flip her attention back to him and away from the dog. "I've spent enough time with dogs to know that they sense things in people, and I've started to understand the signs."

"So you think I should get a dog and let him choose my crew?" she joked.

Logan smiled, but his expression was still serious. "No, I think you need to listen to your gut and trust your own instincts. If it's not him, you'll know."

Well, that was exactly what she'd done by coming here, trusting her gut, and she was already doubting herself.

"This is a nice place you've got," she said, changing the subject.

Tomorrow she'd figure out how to deal with her manager. Tonight, she just wanted to forget all the stuff that had been troubling her for so long. If she was going to start trusting her instincts, then she was going to start with how she felt about Logan.

Candace looked around, liking the white hall and the open-plan living space she could see into. Logan motioned for his dog to move away, and they all walked through the house.

"Have you lived here for long?" she asked.

Logan crossed the room to the fridge and she sat at one of the high-backed chairs at the counter that split the living room from the kitchen.

"I purchased this place soon after my parents died, but I'm not sure if I'll keep it."

He held up a beer and a bottle of water, and she pointed to the water.

"Are you planning on going back to your ranch?"

Logan shrugged. "I want to spend a lot of time there, but I haven't really decided what to do with myself. Once this job is finished, I should officially be discharged for retirement from the army, and so will Ranger."

She smiled when he passed her the water and she opened it, taking a sip. "I'm guessing you get to keep him?"

"Yeah. That grey muzzle of his means he's done his time. He's worked as hard as any human soldier since he was a couple years old, but the stress and discipline eventually gets to them, just like it does us. I paid to get him home, and my parents actually started a foundation to make sure working military dogs receive the retirement they deserve."

"I love feel-good stories like that. Working for charity means a lot to me."

They were silent a while, Logan standing with his beer in hand, looking at his dog, and Candace looking around at his home. She knew that soldiers didn't earn a heap of money, and his house was furnished beautifully in a masculine kind of way, which was making her realize that his family must have been relatively well off. It shouldn't have mattered, but it made her curious about who he was and why he'd spent so many years in the army if he hadn't had to, financially.

"Logan, why did you take me out for dinner tonight?" she asked, unable to keep the question to herself.

His dark eyes locked on hers, sending goose pimples across her skin, making every part of her body tense.

"There was something about you that reminded me of myself," he said, his voice an octave lower than it had been before. "I liked you, and I guess I also wanted to show you that you could just spend a night out in Sydney like a regular woman. But it kind of backfired in the end, because we never even made it to a bar."

Candace swallowed, not sure where her confidence was coming from but suddenly needing to know more, wanting to know what Logan thought of her. She knew it was needy, that she should have just shut up, but the way he was looking at her, the way she was reacting to him, was more than just platonic.

"So this wasn't technically a date?" she asked, dropping her gaze and fiddling with the label on her water bottle.

"Do you want this to be a date?" he asked straight back.

Candace didn't look up, not straightaway, but she heard Logan move, his boots echoing out against the timber floor until he was standing beside her. He reached for her bottle and pulled it away, sliding it across the counter just out of her reach. Then he took her hand, his palm closing over it, waiting for her to respond.

She forced herself to raise her chin, to meet his stare.

"Candace?"

"I don't know," she whispered, her voice cracking. "I honestly don't know."

"Do you want this?" he asked, bending slightly, his mouth stopping barely inches from hers.

Candace didn't say anything, *couldn't say anything,* because as badly as she knew she should say no, she wanted it. Her body was humming like an electric current was running through it, all her senses firing to life, desperate to connect with Logan.

He paused for what felt like an eternity, before cupping her cheek and touching his lips so gently to hers that she almost didn't feel it. His lips hovered, pressed lightly, before his entire mouth moved against hers. She matched his pace, loving the feel of his warm, soft lips, the touch of his palm against her skin.

Candace sighed as he pulled back, like he was giving her the chance to change her mind, and she reached for his shirt, pulling him back toward her. His mouth was

firm to hers again, tongue softly teasing hers, desire
making her stomach flip with excitement as Logan's
hands skimmed her waist before settling on her hips.
His fingers were still then, the only part of his body
moving was his lips, and Candace wanted more. She
was hungry for him, craving the kind of contact she'd
avoided for so long.

Candace ran her hands down Logan's chest until she
reached the hem of his T-shirt, slowly touching beneath
it, connecting first with the waistband of his jeans and
then with bare skin. She let her fingertips explore his
rock-hard abs, the warmth of his skin and the hardness
of his muscles, making her moan into his mouth.

She had half expected him to pull back, to tell her
no, but there was nothing about Logan's body language
that was saying *no*. His hands matched hers, disappearing under her top and touching *her* bare skin, the
slightly rough edge of his fingertips making the sensa-
tion even more erotic.

"Logan," she moaned, knowing she should stop but
giving it only a fleeting thought.

His mouth became more insistent, crushing her lips
before he started kissing down her neck, to her collar-
bone, his tongue tracing across the tops of her breasts.

Candace fisted her hand in his short hair, fingernails
scraping his scalp.

"You want me to stop?" he mumbled, lifting his head
to look into her eyes.

She shook her head. "No."

Logan didn't need any further encouragement. His
mouth met hers in a wet, erotic kiss, before he scooped

her up into his arms as if she were weightless, carrying her through the kitchen, marching down the hall.
Candace sighed against his mouth, her lips moving in a
lazy movement in time with his, their kiss less intense
now but still making her belly flutter with anticipation.

It had been so long since she'd kissed a man, since
she'd been intimate, and instead of being scared of it
like she'd thought she would be, she could feel only a
burning sense of desire. That even though she'd never
had a one-night stand in her life, been with a man she
wasn't in a committed relationship with, there wasn't
a bone in her body that didn't want this right now. She
was always the good girl, the one who stayed out of
the media and never made a wrong step, but she was
on the other side of the world with a man who'd shown
more interest in keeping her away from the limelight
than trying to be in it himself. So if she was going to do
something reckless, then why not with Logan?

She'd tried marriage, tried settling down, and it had
been disastrous. But this? This felt right in every way
possible.

"Candace, we don't have to do this," he mumbled,
walking with her in his arms until he could set her on
the bed.

"I want this," she whispered as he covered her
body with his, her legs looping around his waist so he
couldn't get away, locking him in place.

"I'm not going to ask you again, but I will stop if
you ask me to," he told her, propping himself up on his
elbows and looking down at her, his hazel-brown eyes

like pools of the darkest chocolate in the half-light. "You just say the word, and I'll stop, okay?"

Candace nodded, suddenly feeling vulnerable with this gorgeous, big man lying on top of her, yet being so careful with her at the same time. The last man she'd been with had never put her first, had hurt her with his mind and with his fists, which made her even more attracted to Logan. The fact that he was so strong yet so gentle told her that she'd been right to trust herself, at least in spending one night with him. In letting him be the first man to get close to her since her divorce.

"Thank you, Logan," she whispered.

His eyebrows shot up. "For what?"

"For just letting me be me tonight."

He dropped a slow, careful kiss to her forehead. It shouldn't have, but it felt more intimate than all the touches, all the kisses, they'd already shared.

"I haven't been me in a long time, Candace, so this is a first for me, too."

She had the feeling like they were two lost souls who'd found one another, two people who'd crossed paths for a reason, if only for one night. Logan had shared some of what he'd been through with her, and she'd hinted at her past, too—just enough so they both understood that they were the way they were for a reason.

Logan stared at her, his gaze unwavering, until she arched her body, stretching up to catch his mouth, to start the dance that they'd started in the kitchen. His gaze went from thoughtful to something that scared and excited her in equal parts, his mouth insistent, his hands even more so as he pushed up her top, sliding it up high so he could touch her stomach and then her breasts, his fingers teasing her nipples through the lace bra she was wearing.

Candace was just as desperate for him, wanting his bare skin against hers, needing to feel his naked body pressed to her own. She wanted Logan to make love to her, and she wanted it now.

Logan was trying hard to hold back, to let Candace set the pace and not push her, but after months serving overseas and hardly even *seeing* a woman, having Candace beneath him was sending him stir-crazy. She had a body like he'd never touched before—her waist was tiny, her limbs long and slender, and her breasts... He stifled a groan. They were full and luscious, and he wanted them free from the scrap of lace she had them covered with.

When she arched her body into him this time, her chest pressed to his, he took his chance to reach behind her and unhook her bra. He wanted to touch her, taste her, feel every part of her. And his impatience was starting to get the better of him. It wasn't often he could block everything out—his past, the memories—but with Candace, right now he couldn't think of anything else.

"Candace, you're so beautiful."

Her shy smile spurred him on even more because it was so unexpected.

"You're sure you want this?" He had to ask, needed

to make sure she'd thought this through. "I don't want you to regret anything in the morning."

Candace reached for him, cupped her hands around the back of his head and pulled him lower, her lips warm and pillowy as they traced his mouth.

"No regrets, Logan," she murmured. "I want you to make love to me."

Logan groaned as one of her hands left his neck, her fingernails trailing lightly down his skin, pushing at his jeans like she was as impatient as he was.

This time, he wasn't holding back, wouldn't push her away or ask her if she was sure. He'd given her a chance to say no, and she'd made it perfectly clear what she wanted. Now, he was going to give her exactly what she'd asked for.

Logan stroked Candace's long hair, gently fingering the curls that were splayed across his chest. They'd been lying in silence for a while, just lying in the dark. It wasn't a silence he wanted to break, either—she seemed as comfortable as he was with saying nothing at all, bodies pressed together, his fingers caressing either her hair or her skin.

He shut his eyes, starting to drift into sleep.

The sound of a plane's engine, the dark silence as it stalled and started to spiral, falling toward the earth.

Logan blinked and went back to stroking Candace's hair, touching a strand of it to his face as he focused on her again and stamped the dark thoughts away. He was not going to ruin this perfect moment with lurching back into the past.

"Logan, can I ask you something?" Candace's words were soft and husky.

He stopped twirling her hair and brushed his knuckles softly across her cheek as he propped on one elbow to look at her. She was lying on her back, and now he was on his side, facing her. Staring into her eyes seemed to help him to forget everything else.

"You seem to find it easy to talk about some of the things you've been through, and I guess I…" Her voice trailed off. "I guess it's just unexpected from someone who's been through what you've been through."

Logan wanted to look away but he didn't. "What I've told you is a very small part of what I've been through, Candace. There are some things I'll take to my grave that I should probably talk about but never will, and other things that I *can* talk about for reasons I don't understand." What he didn't tell her was that his head so was full of his memories that he wouldn't even know where to start.

She reached for his hand and linked her fingers with his. "So why did you tell me what you did, about being on patrol, being recognized, all those stories?"

He dropped his gaze to their hands, craving the contact, the touch of her skin to his. "There's something about you that reminds me of, well, me," Logan tried to explain. "I've been through a lot, and I saw something in you that made me want to talk to you. I don't know why. I've never wanted to before, but…"

She turned and snuggled into him. "You don't have to explain. I shouldn't have asked."

Logan dropped a kiss to her forehead, moving to her lips when she tilted her face up to him.

"That's the crazy thing. I'm usually so protective over my past, yet with you I wanted to talk." It was strange, because she also helped him to forget.

She laughed, just a soft, husky giggle. "Yeah, that's probably because you know enough about me to hold me for ransom over your secrets."

Logan raised his eyebrows. "Meaning I could sell all our sex secrets and whispered conversations to the media?"

"Exactly," Candace confirmed.

Logan just smiled and pulled her into him, lying back on the bed and shutting his eyes. He didn't need to say anything in response, because if she didn't trust him, it wasn't something she'd joke about. And there was no way he'd ever spill the beans on anything about Candace, or any other woman he'd ever been with, for that matter.

The last woman he'd shared his own bed and memories with, so many years ago, had hurt him beyond belief. She'd betrayed him when he'd trusted her, made him wary of any other woman and what she could do to him if he let her close. But Candace, she was different, because she felt she had too much to lose to betray him, or his confidence.

It might only be one night, he might never see her again, but it had been worth it. Because Candace had shown him that he wasn't the only damaged person in the world, and it had done him good to see the world through someone else's eyes for once. Or maybe it was because he knew it was only one night that he'd allowed anything to happen at all.

Candace lay awake, her head on Logan's shoulder, hand resting on his chest. She was listening to his breathing, feeling the gentle rise and fall of his chest, as she thought about what she'd just done. She had no regrets and doubted she would, but there were so many things running through her mind that she knew she'd never be able to fall asleep, even if she was exhausted.

Logan had shown her what it was like to just be a woman attracted to a man. She had no intention of making one-night stands a habit, and it wasn't like she'd ever had one before, but tonight had been...just what she'd needed. Her body was relaxed and satisfied, but her mind was working in overdrive, thinking about all the things she needed to do to get her life and her career back on track. And what he'd said about her manager—she didn't want it to be true, but Logan's words had made her wonder. Deep down, she wasn't even that surprised, in fact, if it was true she'd almost be relieved that there wasn't some psycho out there wanting to kill her! Ever since her mom had passed away, she'd ignored the fact that she no longer had someone she could trust in her life, to make all the big decisions for her.

But she was also thinking about the fact that she needed a getaway plan—she'd probably never see Logan again, and she didn't want things to be awkward between them when he woke up. Better to have a beautiful memory of what had happened than an awkward parting, or at least that's what she was thinking as she lay beside him.

"No!"

Candace jumped, pushing away from Logan as his body convulsed. She pulled the sheets up to cover her naked body, eyes trained on the man she'd just been cuddled up to. She'd been lying in the almost dark for so long that her eyes were fully adjusted, and she could see the sweat that had broken out across Logan's forehead, his hands clenched at his sides like he was about to start a fight. What the hell was happening?

"No!"

His voice was loud this time, the order clear, and Candace had shivers working like propellers down her spine, the familiar taste of fear like bile in her mouth. She knew it was a dream, probably a night terror that had something to do with what he'd been through, but she was still scared. Because she'd seen a violent man up close and personal, and it had terrified her.

What if he hurt her? Candace jumped clear off the bed. A whining noise made her spin, her heart still racing, but she realized it was only Ranger, and he had absolutely zero interest in her. He had run to Logan, was sitting beside the bed, head cocked to the side, emitting a low whine. Maybe he was used to his master's behavior? Or maybe he was just as scared by what was happening as she was.

Candace knew it was stupid, but she also knew what it was like to be on the receiving end of a man's fist, of being hurt by someone she'd never expected to hurt her, so she wasn't going to stay too close to Logan. And she definitely wasn't going to risk waking him. She'd seen enough television shows about soldiers with post-traumatic stress to know she could end up with his hands wrapped around her throat if he mistakenly thought she was the enemy.

"I'm sorry, Logan," she whispered, dressing in the dark as he continued to toss and turn, the sheets starting to tangle around him. She should have tried to help him, but she didn't, *couldn't*.

Candace found her shoes, slipped them on, then disappeared out into the living area. She pulled her phone from her purse, saw she'd missed a heap of calls while it had been on silent, but ignored them all and went online instead. She searched for the name of a taxi company, found out Logan's address, called to order a cab, and sat down on the sofa while she waited.

Running out on Logan wasn't something she'd wanted to do. It wasn't something she'd ever done before to any man, but she'd set the wheels in motion now and there was no turning back. What they'd shared had been incredible, a night she'd never forget for as long as she lived, but they'd made each other no promises, and now it was time to head back to the real world.

Even if right now that world held little appeal.

CHAPTER FIVE

LOGAN STRETCHED AND threw one hand over his eyes to block out the sun. He went to pull the pillow over his head instead before he realized what had woken him.

Bloody phone.

He reached for it, sitting up as he also realized that he was alone in his bed when he should have had a gorgeous blonde tucked up beside him. Where on earth had she gone so early in the morning?

"Hello," he muttered, shutting his eyes again as he hit the pillow.

"Tell me the media have gone crazy and lost their minds?"

Logan groaned as he recognized his best friend, Brett's, voice, before sitting back up again and pulling his jeans on so he could see if Candace was still in the house. He tripped over his dog, who was looking at him like he was the crazy one. He did that a lot lately, especially in the morning, and he had no idea why.

"Logan?"

"Sorry. What have you seen?" He checked the kitchen and living area, before ducking into the bathroom. All empty. *Crap!* How had he managed to sleep through her leaving?

"Oh, you know, just you leaving Nick's Seafood restaurant with Candace-*freaking*-Evans, and then her spotted arriving back at her hotel at about three this morning looking mighty disheveled."

Double crap. Logan swallowed the expletives that he would like to have yelled out. At least it was Brett telling him rather than some stranger confronting him.

"Are you sure she was seen at the hotel?"

His friend laughed. "You mean you lost her? Hey, Jamie, he didn't even know where she was, so they must have gotten the whole one-night stand thing wrong."

Logan grimaced as he listened to Brett call out to his wife. If it was all over the news, then there was little chance of anyone else believing that nothing had happened, and the last thing he wanted was the whole world to know what Candace had been doing the night before. He couldn't care less what anyone said about him, but he knew that she wasn't exactly the kind of woman used to making headlines for being scandalous.

A noise made him look up and Ranger let out a loud bark.

"Look, I spent the day with her yesterday…"

"And the night?" Brett was laughing, like he found the entire thing beyond hysterical.

"Oh, man!" Logan ducked out of sight when he saw that the front of his house was surrounded by a bunch of guys with cameras. The last thing he needed was to be photographed bare-chested in jeans he hadn't even buttoned up properly.

"What?"

"There's bloody paparazzi outside my house. How did they find my place?" Not to mention *why* they'd want a photo of him when they knew Candace wasn't even with him.

"From the fierce looks you gave them last night it's a wonder they wanted to go near you again."

Logan went around the house pulling all the blinds and drapes down so no one could see in.

"Look, she's a sweet girl and we had a nice night together. *End of story.* Now I have to go and make sure she's okay, because she obviously slipped out on me in the night."

Brett laughed again. "Guess that serves Jamie right for telling you it was time to meet a woman. We just didn't expect you to set your sights quite so high."

Logan was usually ready to spar with Brett whenever he became annoying, but today he wasn't going to take the bait. He could deal with his friend later.

"I have to go. I'll call you later."

"I'll email those pics through to you," Brett said. "You know, in case you want to check yourself out."

"Later."

Logan hung up and opened his fridge, pulling out a carton of juice. He managed to take a few sips before curiosity got the better of him, and he grabbed his phone again and checked his emails. Sure enough, Brett had already hit Send, because there was a link waiting for him to click on.

Naughty night out in Australia for America's sweetheart. Candace Evans waves goodbye to good girl reputation with mystery man.

Logan took a deep breath, refusing to let his anger get to him. He clicked through the shots and saw them leaving the restaurant together, a zoomed-in photo of them holding hands, one of them driving away in his car, then hours later Candace running into the hotel, her hair all messed up and one hand held across her face.

It wasn't like they'd actually caught them doing anything, but they'd built a story around nothing and put up a few photos together to try to prove a point. The worst thing was that she'd run from him, and he had no idea why she'd just disappear like that after they'd spent the night together. Had someone sent her the photos and spooked her?

Whatever had happened, he was going to make sure that she was left alone at the press conference this afternoon. Sure, the media might go crazy when they realized he was her bodyguard, but then again they might think they'd made a huge mistake and he'd just been minding her.

Either way, he was heading to the hotel now to see if she was okay.

His phone bleeped again, this time with a text. He flicked through to his messages, anger rising again when he read the words.

Looks like you had an interesting evening. Heads up that the press junket has been cancelled, so you're officially off duty on this one.

Great. Even his boss knew what he'd been up to, or allegedly up to, the night before. And Candace had obviously gone into hiding if she was giving up her afternoon appointment. Still, he was going to see her. If she was still in the country, he'd track her down. What Candace didn't know about him was that he wasn't exactly a one-night stand kind of guy, either, and he wanted her to know that he'd be there for her if she needed him, until her flight out.

Candace had made him see that he needed to move on with parts of his life that he'd ignored for so long, and for that alone he needed to thank her. Usually when he freaked out over anything, he went for a run or hit the gym. In fact, he usually did it every morning because his dreams freaked him out night after night, but today was different. Today he actually had to confront the problem head-on instead of try to outrun it.

Candace stared at her laptop screen. She was a sucker for punishment, and she still couldn't help clicking through and looking at each photo one more time. She'd looked before her shower, and now she was sitting on her bed, hair wrapped in a towel, torturing herself again.

She felt like a fool.

Being with Logan wasn't something she regretted, even if she did regret the paparazzi getting snaps of her and making it clear to the world what she'd been up to. It was the fact that it had taken Logan's comments for her to realize how bad her manager was—she'd hidden behind the fact that her mom wasn't around any longer, instead of dealing with something she knew was detrimental to her career. But those days were gone. The first thing she'd done in the taxi was text her manager and tell him she was okay, that she would be arriving back at the hotel within twenty minutes, and then when she'd arrived to quietly slip into her room, the place had been buzzing with photographers. There was only one explanation for it, and she was going to be giving him his marching orders and sending him packing before the end of the day, after she asked him whether he was responsible for the letters she'd been receiving.

Then she was going to figure out how to apologize to Logan for running out on him in the middle of the night, before figuring out what to do for the next few days. It was time for her to take a break, figure some things out, and find a beach to relax on where she wouldn't be disturbed. She didn't have any more concerts scheduled on this tour, and she'd been too busy for too long without taking time out for herself, punishing herself with work to avoid dealing with everything that had happened.

Her hotel phone rang but she ignored it, uninterested in whoever it was. She'd made it clear she didn't want to be disturbed, and she meant it.

Candace padded barefoot back into the bathroom and let her hair down, running her fingers through it and then working some product into the roots. She would do her hair and makeup, then deliver the verdicts that she'd decided upon.

It was time for her to take control of her own life, her own destiny, and that started today.

CHAPTER SIX

"LOGAN, IT'S CANDACE."

He stopped dead, flicking his phone off speaker and pressing it to his ear instead.

"Candace? I thought you were long gone."

There was silence for a moment, and Logan had to check that they hadn't lost the connection. The last thing he'd expected was for Candace to call.

"I was wondering if you had time to meet up," she asked, her voice low.

"Business or pleasure?" Logan cringed the second the words left his mouth. *Pleasure* hadn't exactly been the best phrase, given what had happened between them.

"Coffee," she said. "I'm at a different hotel, just down the road from where I was before."

"I can't believe you're still in Australia." *Unbelievable.* Almost two days later and he'd been sure he'd never hear from her again, especially when she'd never answered her door when he'd known she was in her room that next morning.

"You're still here, in Sydney, right? I mean, I thought you might have already left for the Outback."

"I leave tomorrow," he told her. "I'll head to you now, if that's okay with you?"

"Sure. Meet me in an hour at my hotel. I'll be in the café, and I'm wearing a short brown wig."

Logan said goodbye, zipped his phone into his pocket and tapped his thigh as a signal to Ranger. It would take him at least fifteen minutes to run home if he sprinted, but given that he was about to cut his workout short, he wasn't complaining. Ranger bounded along beside him and Logan tried not to overthink the phone call he'd just received.

He wasn't going to even bring up what had happened between them unless she did, and he was most definitely not going to offer to help her or take her out again. She had a bunch of professionals at the ready if she needed them, and he was done with the army and with working any kind of security, at least for now. From next week onward, he was just Logan Murdoch, civilian. He was going to spend time on the land, forget about the future for a while, and figure stuff out.

Or at least that was the plan.

He blanked everything out of his mind, focusing only on the soles of his shoes as they thumped down on the pavement. Logan concentrated on each inhale and exhale of breath, the pull and release of his muscles, his dog matching his pace as he ran directly at heel.

Exercise was how he kept in control, how he stayed focused, and it was the only constant he'd had in his life for a very long time. Candace might have rattled him, but he was going to stay in control and not let anyone distract him. And that included her.

Candace's legs were so fidgety she was fighting the urge to get up and start to pace. But then that would have only drawn attention to herself, and the whole point of sitting quietly and wearing her brunette disguise was so no one even thought to glance twice at her.

She still didn't know exactly what she was going to say to Logan, but starting off by thanking him for being so honest with her about her management team, and then apologizing for disappearing on him, was probably a good starting point. The guy had been nothing but nice to her, and he deserved an explanation about what had happened between them, and for how right he'd been about Billy. He'd set her on the right path and he deserved to know.

"Candace?"

She turned when a deep, low voice said her name. Heat flooded her body when she saw Logan, standing with his hands jammed into his jean pockets. There had never been any doubting that he was incredibly sexy, but seeing him in the flesh again brought back a certain amount of memories that she'd been trying to repress. Namely his mouth, his rock-hard abs, his…

Candace jumped up and kissed Logan on the cheek, stamping out those thoughts. "Hey."

"Wow, you look…" He hesitated. "Different."

"I don't know if I'm fooling the hotel staff, but so far no one has bothered me," she admitted. "It won't last long, but I'm planning on checking out first thing tomorrow."

Logan went to sit down, then stopped. "You want a coffee?"

Candace glanced at her empty cup. "Another chai latte would be great."

She watched as he crossed the room to order, rather than waiting for someone to come and serve them, before sitting down across from her. It was all old-fashioned decadence here, and big, strong Logan looked the completed opposite of the hushed-toned men in suits walking past. He looked relaxed in his jeans and shirt like only a confident, strong man could, and she liked that he had such a strong identity of who he was—or at least that's the impression he gave.

"Logan, I want to apologize for just leaving in the middle of the night. It wasn't something I've ever done before, and you deserved better."

She struggled to read his expression, but he didn't look angry.

"I'm not going to lie. I was looking forward to waking up to you beside me," he said, staring into her eyes and not giving her one chance to look away. "But I get it. You saw the photos and you freaked."

Candace took a slow, deep breath. So he thought she'd seen the pics on her phone and run. That she could live with. If he'd thought she was stone cold and happy to just bed him and then leave? Not something she'd have been able to swallow very easily.

"I'm just sorry that I dragged you into all this. You were just trying to be nice to me and…"

"Stop," he said, reaching for her hand then hesitating, like he'd acted before realizing what he was doing. "We had a great evening together and it didn't end quite as planned. We're both grownups and we never made any promises to one another. Right?"

So in other words he didn't care? Candace pushed aside the feelings of hurt, the emotion clogging her throat. This was why she wasn't a one-night stand regular, because she couldn't handle the blunt truth of a man being honest with her.

"Logan, I wanted to thank you for being honest with me," she started, reminding herself of the real reason she'd wanted to see him. "You were more honest with me than anyone has been in a long while, even though you hardly even knew me."

He raised an eyebrow. "This sounds serious."

She nodded, waiting for their coffees to be placed in front of them before continuing. "I fired my manager and pretty much everyone else I've been working with, and I'm going to take some time off before rehiring anyone. Just be me for a while."

He sat back, gaze fixed on her. "What changed? Why now, after all this time?"

Candace tried to relax, but with Logan staring at her she was finding it hard enough just to focus on breathing and saying what she'd rehearsed in her mind.

"I've used losing my mom as an excuse for too long now, and it wasn't until you read the situation for what it was that I realized I'd been putting things off for too long. I'm sick and tired of letting people make decisions for me, and you were right about everything. I've been

spooked about those letters for so long that it was starting to consume me, and it was my manager all along."
She blew out a deep breath. "All I've ever wanted to do,
all my life, is just sing. But now that Mom's not here to
cover my back for me, I need to step up and take more
control of everything, rather than just burying my head
in the sand."

He reached for his coffee cup and took a sip of the
steaming black liquid. "For the record, I'm not one of
those people who'd ever use you, and I will never talk
to anyone about what happened between us. Or about
the whole manager situation for that matter."

Candace couldn't help it—suddenly her eyes filled
with tears and she was reaching for a napkin to blot
them away.

"Candace?"

Logan was suddenly at her side, moving to the chair
next to hers, his arm around her.

"Candace, please don't cry."

She shook her head and blinked the tears away, refusing to turn into an emotional mess.

"I'm sorry, it's just I'm not used to…" Her voice
trailed off. "*You.* The way you are with me."

Logan kept his arm around her, and when she turned
to him she could see confusion in his expression.

"I'm not sure what you mean?"

Candace looked up at the bright lights above, wishing she knew how to tell him what she meant.

"I'm not used to a straight talker, and I'm sure as
heck not used to being with someone who doesn't have
an ulterior motive. Who won't sell me out to the press."

She shrugged. "I'm just so tired of watching my back and not knowing who to trust, especially after what I've been through the past few weeks. I've been scared for so long, looking over my shoulder all the time, and it was just a ploy to create more press about me. Press that I didn't even want."

They were silent, just sitting there, Logan not saying anything in response for what felt like an eternity.

"Candace, I'm heading out with a couple of friends tonight. Why don't you join us?"

She knew she must have looked wide-eyed, but she could hardly believe what she was hearing.

"You mean to say you'd actually go out in public with me again? After what happened last time?"

Now it was Logan shrugging. "Look, it's no big deal. You can even wear your wig if you like. We'll just be heading to a bar for a few drinks, nothing too exciting, and I doubt we'll even be noticed if we're careful."

Logan dropped his arm and moved back around to his seat, his coffee cup in his hand again.

"You're sure your friends won't mind?"

"Brett has been my best mate for years, and I've known his wife almost as long. We're just hanging out for some drinks before I leave tomorrow. Catching up for a few hours."

Candace stared into her latte, wishing she'd been brave enough to just say yes from the start.

"If you're sure…"

Logan had no idea where that had come from. Why had he even asked her? The plan had been to see her, listen to what she had to say, then walk away. What happened to her not being his problem? To her not being part of his life? To not letting anyone too close?

"I'm sure," he heard himself say. "It'll be fun."

The words were just falling out of his mouth now like he had absolutely zero control over the link between his brain and his vocal cords, and that definitely wasn't something he was used to. He usually found it harder to talk than not.

"If anyone recognizes me or it becomes awkward, I'll just leave."

"Candace, it'll be fine. Want to meet me there or should I swing past and collect you?"

"If you wouldn't mind coming to get me?"

Her voice was low, a shyness there that made his protective instincts flare up, and told him exactly why he'd asked her. He liked her, sure, was beyond attracted to her, but he was also able to sense the vulnerability that for some reason she wasn't great at hiding around him. Anyone who saw her on stage or in public would think she was full of confidence, but he'd already seen firsthand that there was a lot more to Candace than met the eye.

"I'll pick you up at eight," he said.

Logan rose, unable to take his eyes off her. Even with a pair of crazy-high heels on she was still short beside him, and part of him just wanted to tell her to grab her things and come with him now so he could look after her. But he didn't. Because he had things to arrange for the morning, paperwork to deal with, and because he *did not* want to get involved.

Spending the night with a woman he'd never expected to see again had been one thing, but he knew he wasn't ready for anything else. There wasn't enough room in his mind or his heart to worry about another human being, to give what someone like Candace deserved. And besides, it wasn't like she'd indicated that she wanted anything else, either.

They could have another fun night together, and then they'd say goodbye for real.

"Thanks, Logan," Candace said, suddenly reaching out for him, her palm soft against his forearm as she stopped him from walking away. "After everything, just, thanks."

She didn't let go of him straightaway, and they stared at one another, not moving. Logan clenched his jaw as memories of their night together came flooding back to him—her hands on his skin, her body against his as he'd traced every part of her with his mouth and fingers. This girl.... God! She was under his skin and no matter what he tried to tell himself, being this close to her made it impossible not to want her.

"I'll see you tonight," he said, clearing his throat when he heard how husky his voice sounded.

"See you tonight," she repeated, slowly releasing him and taking a step back.

Logan gave her one last look, hesitated one second too long. Before he could even think through what he was doing, he'd closed the distance between them again, wrapping his arm around her so he could put his hand flat to the small of her back, lips closing over hers. It was a hungry kiss that he hadn't even known he'd been waiting to plant on her mouth, and she didn't disappoint. Candace kissed him back like she was as hungry for contact as he was, before raising her hand and placing it on his chest to push him back slightly.

"The purpose of the wig was to *not* draw attention to myself," she whispered, eyes dancing as she stared up at him.

Logan chuckled, shaking his head. What had Candace done to him? So much for being the guy Brett called Mr. No Emotion. He'd gone years without having any issues of self-control around the opposite sex, and now he was behaving like a deprived addict.

"I'll try to be on my best behavior tonight," Logan muttered.

Candace stroked his face, gently, like she was touching something fragile. She didn't, *couldn't,* know it, but that was exactly what he was. No one else saw it—everyone treated him based on his physical appearance and based on the rank he held—when inside he knew he was as vulnerable, if not more so, than anyone else. He just hoped she couldn't see too much of who he was, because he was certain the darkness of his thoughts, his memories, would send her running.

"I'll see you at eight," he said.

Logan backed away and turned, walking in a straight line toward the lobby and the front doors. This time he made it to his car, unlocking the vehicle and jumping behind the wheel. Ranger nudged him, dancing from paw to paw in excitement at not being left alone for too long.

"Don't ask," Logan muttered, giving the dog's head a scratch.

What he should have been concerned about was how much he was starting to treat Ranger like a pet instead of an elite military dog, and how easily they'd fallen into bad habits since they'd been home. Instead he was thinking about a blonde who'd looked just as sexy as a brunette, and who was starting to drive him crazy.

He picked up his phone and dialed Brett, hitting speaker and putting his phone on his lap.

"All set for tonight?" Brett said as he answered.

Logan fought the urge to thump his head on the steering wheel. Instead he yanked on his seat belt and started driving, needing to be distracted.

"There's been a slight change of plan," he told Brett.

"Don't even think about it. Jamie will kill you if you cancel."

"I'm not cancelling. I'm, ah, bringing someone."

Logan waited for the laughter, but all he heard was silence.

"Anyone I know?"

"Look, I need you guys to just not make a fuss. Just treat her like any other girl I might have met and brought along for a drink."

"Except you've never brought a girl along before," Brett said with a laugh. "In fact, I don't know when I last heard the words Logan and date uttered in the same sentence."

"I'm warning you…" Logan told him, knowing he could trust his best mate but going all stupid and protective over Candace anyway.

"No need. It'll be fun. Want to just meet us there?"

"Yeah, I'll see you there."

Logan hung up and let his head fall back against the rest. Asking Candace out had been crazy, but the fact he was heading out with Brett and Jamie would mean there was no pressure, that everything would be fine. So long as he didn't end up taking her back to his place again, it would just be a night out with friends.

Ranger whined and Logan took his eyes off the road for a split second to glare at him.

"I know, I know, but it's only one night."

His dog ignored him and stared out the window, and Logan tried to think about going back home to the Outback instead of what the night was going to be like. Because he couldn't convince his dog, and he couldn't convince himself that seeing Candace for a few hours over a drink was ever going to be enough. Or that he'd be able to hold back and not end up trying to make something happen between them again.

Weakness wasn't something he'd ever struggled with before. He'd had to fight a lot of other emotions, deal with loss and a lot of crap over the years, but no one could ever have accused him of being weak. Until a gorgeous, sexy country singer had walked into his life and turned everything he'd ever known, ever felt, up on its head.

Next thing he knew he'd be playing her music and singing along to her songs like a lovesick puppy.

Candace had a pile of rejected clothes strewn across the bed. After trying almost everything on, she'd settled on a pair of skinny jeans, a T-shirt with sequined sleeves and a pair of super-high stilettos. Logan was insanely tall and while she liked the fact that his size made her feel protected, she didn't like only reaching his shoulder if her shoes weren't high enough.

She fluffed her hair, tousling her curls, and applied one final brush of lip gloss. Candace was about to reach for her purse when her phone beeped. She grabbed it and scrolled through her emails, smiling when she read the first new message.

Candace Evans spotted getting cozy with mystery man in L.A.? Source sees her being rushed through customs and into the arms of another stranger.

She blew out a sigh of relief and flicked her phone to silent before jamming it into her purse. Her tip-off had worked, which meant no one would be expecting her to still be in Australia, and definitely not at a local bar hanging out with some regular people. She just had to hope that enough gossip sites passed around the message.

Candace left the light on in her room and turned the message on the door to Do Not Disturb, then headed for the elevator. Her heart was pounding, nerves making her hands damp. The anticipation of seeing Logan again was putting her more on edge than she ever was just before a concert. It was crazy, and she hadn't been like this around a guy for a very long time, but something about the sexy soldier-turned-bodyguard had her stomach doing cartwheels.

She'd promised herself that she wouldn't ever fall for a man again, that she was better off being single, but while that might have been easy before, it didn't seem quite so straightforward now. Because Logan had shown her that not all men were jerks, and no matter how hard she wanted to resist him, her willpower had failed her from the moment she'd agreed to go out with him the first time.

The elevator dinged and Candace took a deep breath and walked out. She hadn't bothered to put her wig on, but she did keep her head down as she walked toward the lobby doors. She doubted anyone would bother staring at her too hard, and all the excitement over her concert had well and truly died down.

"Candace."

She glanced up just as she almost walked straight into Logan, his deep voice stopping her. He was standing with his arms folded, waiting like he'd kill anyone with his bare hands if they so much as came near her.

"Hey," she said, wishing the sight of him had settled instead of unnerved her.

"I was half expecting a brunette tonight," he joked, turning so he could put his arm around her and walk them both out of the hotel. "It's kind of like the whole Miley Cyrus versus Hannah Montana thing."

His joke blew all the nerves from her body, somehow made her relax.

"How on earth do you know *anything* about Hannah Montana?" she asked, laughing as he opened the door to his vehicle.

Logan leaned in toward her, one arm braced on the

door. "Ten-year-old niece. I was trying to be a good uncle."

Candace laughed to herself as he shut the door. *This* was why she liked Logan so much—being in his company was...refreshing. It made her feel like she was a world away from everything, and right now that was the best feeling she could imagine.

"So tell me about your friends," she said, angling her body so she could stare at Logan. "Do they know you're bringing someone along with you?"

He glanced at her before starting the engine, and she was just watching as his mouth opened to reply when—

"Argh!" Candace squealed and almost hit her head on the ceiling.

"Ranger!" Logan barked, pushing his dog back and reaching for her, his hand covering her thigh. "I'm sorry. I was just about to warn you and then..."

"Your dog stuck his tongue in my ear. Actually in my ear," Candace complained, wiping at her face and glaring at the dog in the backseat. But her anger quickly turned to laughter when she saw the confused look on Ranger's face.

"It's fast becoming one of his party tricks," Logan confessed. "We both apologize, don't we, Ranger?"

Candace reached back and gave the dog a stroke on the head, finding it hard to believe that the dog had actually molested her, not to mention the fact that she was voluntarily touching him.

"It's okay. I guess that was just him saying hi," she said, not wanting to get the dog into trouble now that

she was actually starting to like him. "Next time I sug-
gest warning your passenger, though."

Logan stroked his hand across her thigh before putting it back on the wheel, and she wished she had the
nerve to just grab it and put it back in place.

"He was all upset seeing my bags packed, so I told
him he could tag along for the ride."

Candace leaned back in her seat, keeping an eye on
the dog in case he decided to get frisky again.

"Anyway, you were asking about Brett and Jamie?"

"Yeah. Tell me about them."

Logan made a noise in his throat that made her think
he didn't really want to discuss them, but then he took
one hand off the wheel and seemed to relax.

"Brett is one of my oldest friends. We met our first
day of training, and we both ended up going through
to the SAS and then the doggies division."

"Has he retired now, too?"

Logan nodded. "Yeah, he was injured pretty bad on
his last tour."

She watched as Logan's jaw tightened, a visible tick
alerting her to the fact that this might not be something
he was comfortable discussing with her.

"Is he, ah, one of the guys you mentioned the other
night? One of the two that you used to meet up with at
the restaurant?" Candace hoped she hadn't pushed him
too far by asking.

Logan didn't say anything straight away, but he did
put his fallen hand back on the wheel, the whites of his
knuckles showing how hard his grip was. She wished

she knew what was going through his mind, wondered if it was the same memories that he fought in the night.

"There were three of us. Brett, Sam and me. They were on tour together about a year ago, working a routine patrol, when an IED bomb went off and killed Sam."

Logan paused and Candace just stayed still, silent.

"Brett lost his dog in the blast, too, and he's so lucky to be alive himself."

She had no idea what to say. "Logan, I'm sorry."

He shrugged, but she knew he wasn't finding it easy to talk about, that it wasn't something he'd ever be able to truly shrug off, no matter how convincing he might look.

"When Brett came home, things kind of became difficult between us when he, well, he kind of fell in love with Sam's wife. His widow, I mean. It's all a bit of a complicated story, but at the end of the day it was the best thing for both of them."

Jeez. When Logan had said he'd been through a lot these past few years, he actually had.

"You must have found that pretty hard to deal with?" Candace said. "Understandably so, I mean."

"I was a jerk when I should have listened to them, but Jamie can tell you more about all that if she wants to. All I care about is that they're both happy now." He glanced across at her. "I'm not usually the guy who overreacts, except when it comes to the people I care about."

Candace shifted in her seat as Logan focused on the road again.

"And you," he added, his voice low.

She stopped moving, wondering if she'd heard him right. "Me?" Candace forced herself to ask.

Logan pulled over, parking the car, but she couldn't take her eyes off of him. What did he mean by that?

Once the vehicle was stationary, he turned his body to face hers, reaching for her hand. She let him take it, their fingers linking.

"There's something about you that I can't stay away from, no matter how much I tell myself I should."

Candace was like a spider caught in a web—Logan's gaze was impossible to escape from, and she didn't want to. It was like he was saying the words that were in her head, telling her what she was thinking.

"Meaning you wish you hadn't asked me out tonight?"

"Meaning," he said, cupping her face in his other hand, "that it probably would have been best for both of us if I hadn't, not that I didn't want to."

She knew exactly what he meant, because she'd been telling herself the same thing, knowing that it would have been best to move on and not think about Logan, let alone see him again. But like a bee was lured to nectar time and time again, so it seemed was she to him.

"You're leaving in the morning, right?" she whispered.

Logan nodded, just the barest movement of his head. "Yes."

"Then it's just one more night. We'll both be heading our separate ways tomorrow."

He leaned toward her, placing a feather-light kiss to

her lips. Logan didn't say anything, and he didn't need to. Whatever it was they had between them, whatever was pulling them together, wasn't something either of them seemed to understand. But by tomorrow, neither of them would have a choice.

"Let's go meet your friends," Candace said as he dropped his hand from her face.

Logan smiled and jumped out of the car, and Candace quickly touched up her lip gloss in the mirror.

CHAPTER SEVEN

LOGAN TOOK CANDACE'S hand as they walked toward the entrance of the bar. He hoped no one made a fuss and recognized her, especially not after last time. All he wanted was a quiet evening with friends, a couple of beers and to make the most of his only night left with Candace. So much for telling himself that he was going to play the part of the perfect gentleman tonight. After what she'd said in the car, his mind was all over the "just one more night" line she'd given him.

"They're just over there," he said into her ear, pointing toward where Brett and Jamie were standing near the bar.

Candace squeezed his hand and they headed straight over. He could see the grin on Jamie's face even from across the room once she spotted them, and he knew it wasn't just because it was Candace he'd brought with him. She'd been trying to set him up with someone, *anyone,* for longer than he liked to admit, and even though he'd repeatedly turned her down she'd been pretty insistent that it was time he met someone. Pity he'd have to let her down gently that this wasn't a relationship that was going anywhere.

"Hey!" Jamie said, kissing his cheek and holding her hand out to Candace. "Great to meet you."

Candace smiled and shook hands with both Jamie and Brett, and Logan gave them both a hug.

"What do you want to drink?" Logan asked Candace.

Candace raised her eyebrows and looked at Jamie. "What are you having?"

"A mocktail because I'm driving. But whatever you do, don't let either of these boys talk you into a Long Island Iced Tea."

They all burst out laughing, except for Candace, who just looked confused.

"Come sit down and I'll tell you all about it," Jamie said with a grin, looping her arm through Candace's. "Logan, ask the bartender to make her something delicious. He's good like that."

Logan reached out and touched the small of Candace's back just before she walked away, receiving a sweet smile in response when she glanced over her shoulder. He stared at her as she moved, watched the gentle sway of her body, the long curly hair that hung like a wave down her back and that he was desperate to fist his hands in.

"Hey," Brett said, nudging him in the ribs. "You going to get these drinks or do I have to?"

Logan snapped out of it and stared at Brett.

"I'm losing it," he admitted. "I'm losing the plot and there's nothing I can do about it."

Brett sighed and leaned across the bar to order the

drinks, clearly deciding he was useless for the time being. "Next round's on you," he muttered.

"Brett, I'm serious. She's done something to me and I can't snap out of it."

"So you like her. What's the big deal?"

Logan put one elbow on the bar to prop himself up. "The fact that she's way out of my league, not to mention she leaves tomorrow." He ran a hand through his short hair. "And you know me, I'm just not interested in being with anyone after, well, everything."

Brett chuckled and passed him a beer. "You can pretend all you like, but you're interested in being with her. Otherwise you wouldn't be telling me all this. Besides, you can't dwell on the past forever, no matter how bad it is. At some point you're going to have to move on."

Logan raised the beer bottle and drained almost half of it. "She's under my skin. I want her but I don't, and…"

He had no idea what he was trying to say, because he didn't even know what he wanted. It was impossible to even think straight with her around. Deep down, he doubted he could give enough of himself to any woman, certainly not Candace, but he knew he was starting to think about her as more than a one-night thing. He'd be lying if he told himself he didn't want more. A lot more.

"Logan, she's a beautiful girl, and you've had fun with her. You telling me you want more than that, or are you just pissed that you can't have her in your bed for a few more nights?"

"Don't talk about her like that. It has *nothing* to

do with me just wanting her in bed." Logan knew he sounded angry, and he was.

"Whoa," Brett said, putting his beer down and holding up both hands. "I was just trying to make a point. You don't have to bite my head off."

"Well, don't," Logan grumbled, even though he knew it was him who'd been in the wrong.

"You remember when I was first with Jamie, and I tried to tell you how I felt about her?"

"Was that before or after I gave you the black eye?"

Brett punched him in the arm, but he was still grinning. "The point is, I felt differently about Jamie than I'd ever felt about another woman. I could have lost you as a friend just for telling you, for trying to explain, but she was worth it. *She's still worth it.*" He shrugged. "Your past is never going to go away, so you're just going to have to deal with it."

Logan watched as Brett glanced across to where the girls were seated, and he angled his body so he could see them, too. They were sitting together, heads bent as they discussed something that made them both burst out laughing. Jamie was one of his closest friends, and he'd been right to think that she'd be perfect for Candace to spend time with. And everything Brett was saying was right, even if it was blunt.

"Don't be so much of a hard head that you lose someone you feel that way about, that's all I'm saying," Brett said, picking up his beer bottle and another mocktail for Jamie. "Jamie was worth fighting for, and that would have been the truth no matter how high the stakes. You just have to decide if Candace is worth the fight, what-ever that fight turns out to be."

Logan collected his drinks and walked beside his friend, knowing he was right. He often kept everything bottled up inside and refused to talk, but telling Brett what he was thinking had been the right thing to do.

"It's about time I told you I'm sorry for being a jerk when you tried to talk to me about Jamie," he admitted. "I should never have been so harsh on you, and every time I see the two of you together I know what an idiot I was. I hope you know that."

Brett just shrugged. "You were looking out for her, I get it. And you've said sorry enough times for me to believe you, so how about we just move on, huh?"

"Yeah, but until now, maybe I didn't know how you really felt. I meant it when I apologized back then, but all of a sudden I actually get it," Logan mumbled, eyes locked on Candace as he headed toward her. "As much as I want to forget about her, to ignore the way I feel…"

"You just can't," Brett finished for him. "Trust me, I get it."

"So what do I do?" he asked just before they reached the table. "What am I supposed to do?"

"Stop overthinking it," Brett said in a low voice. "If it feels right, just go with it. For once in your life switch that part of your brain off and just enjoy the moment."

"Hey," Candace said with a smile as Logan sat down beside her on the leather seat.

The table was tucked away, a low-hanging light cast-ing warm shadows around them in contrast to the dark-ness of the bar.

"Try this and see what you think," Logan told her, sliding the drink across to her.

Candace grinned and leaned forward, at the same time resting her hand on his thigh. Logan stiffened, couldn't help how rigid his body went, like it was on high alert, but if she noticed she never said anything. What Brett had said had been right, trouble was that the last time he'd just lived in the moment, he'd had his heart ripped out and stomped all over. Add to that his fear of losing anyone he actually cared about again, and he was one screwed up individual, he knew.

"So what were you two busy talking about?" Brett asked, kissing Jamie when she turned to face him.

"Oh, you know, just telling Candace some stories about you two," Jamie responded. "It's always fun having someone new to share info with."

"I was telling Jamie about my fear of dogs, and how Ranger decided to make love to my ear with his tongue on the way here."

Logan just shook his head when the other two burst into laughter. He'd hoped they'd just be themselves around Candace, and they were, which was making the whole situation seem…like some sort of double date. They weren't treating her any differently than they would any other girl.

He cleared his throat. "I'm heading back home first thing tomorrow, Jamie, did Brett tell you?"

"Don't tell me you want me to babysit Ranger?" Jamie asked. "Or is that something Candace wants to do now that he's shown his love for her?"

Both Candace and Jamie giggled, and Logan exchanged looks with Brett. His friend was giving him a look he'd only seen when they'd been serving, a look that told him he had to do what he had to do. Before, it had been about war, about making decisions that could affect his entire team, and now it was about putting his own heart on the line and putting himself at risk. Which wasn't something he was comfortable with at all. Now, the decision he made was only going to affect his own life, which was why the whole thing was scaring him.

"What are your plans, Candace? You heading back to the States?" Brett asked, giving Logan a moment to gather his thoughts.

Candace was toying with her straw. She took a delicate sip before answering. "You know, I don't have any definite plans as yet, but I'm planning on staying in Australia for a few more days, maybe longer."

Logan almost choked on his beer. "You are?" He turned so he was staring straight at her.

She glanced across at him, her eyes not settling on his. "Yeah. You kind of convinced me that I needed a break."

"When you said you were going to take some time off, I didn't realize you meant *here.* I figured you were going back to your ranch in Montana."

Suddenly it was like there was just the two of them in the room, that Brett and Jamie weren't even part of the conversation. How had she not mentioned this earlier? Why hadn't he asked her?

"You're going tomorrow, and I didn't want you to feel like…" Her voice trailed off, her sentence unfinished.

"I could have changed my plans," he muttered. If

he'd known there was the chance of spending more time with her, of this being more than a one-night thing… he would have what? He still didn't know how he felt about Candace, what he thought, what he was capable of offering.

"Candace, you should see Logan's property while you're here," Brett said, interrupting them just as Logan was about to tear his hair out. "I know you've probably travelled to a lot of beautiful places, but there's nothing quite like the Outback."

An awkward silence fell over the table. Even the ever bubbly Jamie was quiet, which made the whole situation feel more pressure cooked than it was.

"I'd love to see it one day. I'm sure it's pretty special," Candace said, but she kept her head down, eyes on her cocktail.

"Brett, why don't we go get another round of drinks?" Jamie suggested, standing and tugging on Brett's hand.

"But we haven't even…" He stopped talking and just stood up when Jamie gave him a fierce look that Logan caught from the corner of his eye.

Logan let them leave before turning to Candace. His mind was jumbled, his thoughts all over the place, but he kept thinking about what Brett had said and he realized he didn't want to regret anything when it came to the woman seated beside him. It was time to man up and he knew it.

"You should have told me you were staying in Australia," Logan said, going to reach for her hand then hesitating, before forcing himself to get out of his comfort zone and just do it. "I just presumed you were heading back straightaway."

Candace's hand was warm in his, but her eyes were staring at their connection, not back into his. She was deep in thought and he wanted to know what was going through her head, what she wanted from him.

"Candace?" he asked, wishing he hadn't sounded so angry.

"I didn't want to tell you because I don't even know what this is between us," she said, finally looking up at him. "I couldn't exactly ask you not to go back home, to stay for another few days just to keep me company."

Logan's heart physically felt like it was going to stop. The pain he felt at seeing her eyes swim with tears was too much for him to handle, because it was him hurting her and that wasn't something he'd ever intended on doing.

"I have no idea what this is, either, Candace." It was the truth and he didn't know what else to say.

"A couple of years ago, I made a decision that I was better off alone than with a man in my life," she told him, still letting him hold her hand. "And then I met you, and I forgot all about the promise I'd made myself. I want you to know that I've never had a one-night stand in my life until you, Logan, and I'm fairly certain it's not something I'll ever do again."

Logan stared back at Candace, wondering what on earth she saw in him to make her want to spend any time with him at all. Why she trusted him, why they both seemed able to confide in one another.

"I don't have a lot to offer, Candace, not emotionally. But I'm not ready to say goodbye to you yet."

She leaned into him, her cheek to his chest. Logan circled his arms around her body, held her to him and shut his eyes, wanting to remember what it was like to have the tiny blonde against him. To be with a woman who made him feel things he'd never expected to feel again in his lifetime, to simply have Candace tucked against him. For as long as he lived, he'd never forget her warmth, the vulnerability he'd glimpsed—it was a comfort like he'd never experienced before.

"Come with me tomorrow," he said, his voice low.

Candace went so still he couldn't even feel her breathing.

"You mean that?" she asked, keeping her face to his chest.

Logan blew out a breath, not sure how he'd just ended up inviting a woman he barely knew back to his family home. But he had, and deep down he knew he wanted it more than anything. This time, he wasn't going to let his fears make decisions for him.

"Yeah, I mean it."

Candace eventually sat upright, one of her hands touching his face as she stared into his eyes.

"Screw doing what I think I should," she said, the corners of her mouth tipping up into a smile. "I think it's about time I just do what feels right."

He couldn't have said it better himself. Logan kissed her, forcing himself to keep his mouth soft to hers when all he wanted was to lose control. He usually hated any kind of public affection, but he wasn't exactly be-

having like himself around Candace and there was no
way he was going to *not* kiss her with her looking up
at him like that.

"We leave you guys for, like, ten minutes, and already you're making out like a pair of lovesick teen-
agers."

Logan didn't pull away from Candace immediately,
but when he did he glared at Brett. Trust his friend to
push him in one direction then tease him about it as
soon as Logan followed his instructions. But without
Brett's chat, maybe he would have kept his mouth shut
instead of taking a leap of faith.

"I think that round was supposed to be mine," Logan
muttered, wrapping an arm around Candace and letting
her snuggle under his shoulder.

"Yup. You owe me thirty bucks."

The drive back wasn't long, and in a way Candace
wished it had been. The moment they'd buckled up,
Logan had reached for her hand and held it, and they'd
been like that the entire way back to her hotel. Even
though they hadn't said a word, they hadn't needed to,
and Candace had no idea what she would have said to
him, anyway. They'd kind of said it all at the bar and
the silence between them was comfortable.

"Here we are," Logan announced when he pulled
up outside.

Candace reluctantly let go of his hand, wishing she'd
just suggested they go home to his place.

"Do you want to come up?" she asked.

Logan stared straight ahead for a second, like he

wasn't sure what to say, or was having some sort of battle over what he wanted to say and what he thought he should say.

"I can't leave Ranger the whole night in here, but I'll come up for a little bit," he said.

Candace fought the heat starting to spread into her cheeks, finding it hard to believe that she'd been the one to ask a man up to her hotel room. Spending time with Logan was sure making her do a lot of things for the first time.

She jumped out and they both walked into the lobby, side by side but not quite touching. They headed straight for the elevator, and Candace toyed with the idea of putting her arm around Logan before deciding to just stand still and stop fidgeting.

"So this might sound like a weird question, but how exactly do we get to the Outback?" she asked, hoping that didn't make her sound like a dumb blonde. She had no idea whether it was two hours away or ten, and if she had to prepare for an insanely long drive or not.

"Not silly at all," he said, touching his fingers to hers when the doors opened. "I probably should have explained when I asked you."

"Don't tell me we have to go by bus or something?" She didn't want to sound like a princess, but...

"We fly," he said, stepping back so she could select her floor. "The catch is that I'm the pilot."

Candace spun around, her jaw almost hitting the floor. "No way." Logan sure had a way of surprising her when she least expected it.

He grimaced. "Yes way, but if it makes you feel any

better I've had my private pilot license since I was nineteen, so it's not like I'm trying to clock up flying hours just for experience these days."

She couldn't believe what she was hearing. "And the plane's yours?" she asked.

"It's not that unusual for a large Outback station to have a plane," he told her, clearly trying to be modest. "We have a couple of small helicopters based on-site for mustering, but I keep the plane here a lot of the time so I can go back and forth."

Okay, she thought. Maybe the reason he wasn't easily intimidated by her was because he had a lot more family wealth than he'd ever let on before. Either way it didn't bother her, but it did make her even more intrigued about the man she'd just agreed to go on a mini-vacation with. There was so much about Logan that was still a mystery to her.

"If you're comfortable taking me, I'm comfortable flying with you," Candace told him.

They exited the elevator when they reached her floor, stepping out side by side.

"Just in case you're getting any grand ideas, it's just a nice reliable four-seater, nothing over-the-top, so don't expect reclining chairs or champagne."

She smiled. "I don't care what the plane looks like, just so long as it gets us to where we need to go and safely."

A look crossed his face, either sadness or anger, she just couldn't quite put her finger on it, but something changed in him at that exact moment.

"We'll get there," he said in a quiet voice that she hadn't heard before. "Don't you worry about that."

Candace wasn't sure what she'd said, but something had rattled him, she could sense it. She wasn't going to pry, though—if he wanted to talk about something that was troubling him, then he could bring it up when he was good and ready. She hated being pushed when something was on her mind.

"So will I have Ranger strapped in beside me?" Candace asked as she swiped her room key. "Or will I be relegated to the back so he can have your wingman seat?"

Logan chuckled. "He's a seasoned flier after all the miles he clocked up in the army, so you don't have to worry about him turning into a quivering mess and wanting to sit on your knee. He knows his place in the back with his harness on."

They walked into the room and Candace dropped her key and purse onto the side table before flopping down onto the bed.

"Talk about a cheap date. Two cocktails and I'm buzzing."

Logan sat beside her, his thigh grazing hers. "So what did you think of my friends? They weren't too full-on?"

Candace lay back on the bed, kicking off her stilettos. "You're kidding me? They were fantastic. Jamie was hilarious, just the kind of company I've been missing. I really liked her."

"Yeah, she's a great girl." Logan was silent for a while, obviously thinking something over, when he suddenly turned to her. "Candace, I want you to know that I've never taken anyone I've been involved with to my family home before."

Candace went still, staring at the ceiling fan before pulling herself up and sitting back against the pillows. "You haven't?"

He shook his head. "I was dating someone a while back, someone I thought I was going to marry, but my parents died before I had the chance to take her there. I haven't been seriously involved with anyone since."

"I'm sorry," Candace said, wishing she could think of something more helpful to say and coming up with nothing.

"When they died, we'd already gotten engaged, and I was so angry that she hadn't met them, that we hadn't spent time together as a family. It seemed so stupid that I'd never made the time to take her home when it should have been a priority."

"So what happened?" Candace asked, her voice deliberately low.

Logan kicked off his boots and moved up the bed, lying beside her, his head almost touching hers. She waited, hardly breathing she was trying to stay so quiet.

"I've experienced a lot of loss, it's just part and parcel of what I've always done for a job, but losing my parents?"

Candace moved her hand so it was touching Logan's, her fingers linking with his, letting him know she was there for him.

"I still don't know how I managed to pull through.

And then the fiancée I thought was in love with me turned out to be a gold digger."

Now that was something she understood all too well, and why she rarely trusted her instincts when it came to men anymore.

"I don't know what to say, but I can say that I've been in that same position with a couple of men before. Nothing hurts more than that kind of betrayal."

Logan squeezed her fingers. "To be honest, that's why I'm telling you," he said. "Charlotte made a few comments that made me suspicious, that made my friends question her real motives, and so I told her that my parents had been in debt and there wasn't any inheritance left over once the debtors had been paid."

Candace sighed. "Don't tell me. She left straightaway?"

"Yep, she was gone from my life faster than I could blink. Her stuff was moved out of our city house within the week," Logan said, moving so he could put his arm around her. "So I lost my parents and my fiancée within a few weeks of each other."

Candace turned, too, so she could snuggle back into Logan. She'd been thinking about getting him into bed ever since he'd kissed her in the bar, but now that they were here, all she wanted was to lie in his arms. The fact that he trusted her enough to confide in her meant more to her than anything, especially when on so many levels she understood what he'd been through.

"Better to have her walk out before you were married, or after you'd had children. I know it's kind of a cliché to say that, but it's true."

Logan's hand tucked under her breast, keeping her close, the warmth from his body making her want to shut her eyes and just enjoy someone holding her, making her feel wanted.

"Logan, I don't know a lot about Australia, but I'm guessing your ranch is kind of, well, impressive," Candace said. "You're obviously in a—" she struggled to find the right word "—*comfortable* position."

Logan's breath was hot against her ear when he chuckled. "You want to know my net worth before you agree to spending more time with me? Is that what you're saying?"

Now it was Candace laughing. "I couldn't care less how much money you have, but from the story you've just told me I have a feeling you're a more eligible bachelor than you've let on."

"If I'm honest with you, we have one of the biggest privately owned Outback stations in New South Wales, and my sister and I inherited everything jointly," he told her. "It's something I'm proud of, but at the same time I'd rather slip under the radar without anyone taking any notice of me, if you know what I mean."

"And yet you've dedicated the last, what, ten years to the army?"

"Something like that," he said, his mouth against her hair. "I just wanted to prove myself, make my own mark on the world before I took over the day-to-day running of the station. It made my dad proud, and I'd always planned on working side by side with him once I'd finished with the SAS."

Candace kept her eyes shut, loving the feel of Logan

stroking her hair, running his fingers gently through her curls before starting at her scalp again.

"What Charlotte did to me, it screwed me up where women are concerned. I'm not the guy who'll ever settle down, because I couldn't ever trust anyone that much again."

That made her eyes pop open. It wasn't that she had any illusions about Logan wanting to marry her, but the fact that such a nice, genuine man was too afraid of being hurt to love again? It made her sad. She often had similar thoughts, but to actually believe that falling in love would never happen? That wasn't something she believed, no matter how disillusioned she felt sometimes.

"Logan, you deserve to have children one day, to carry on your family's legacy and be happy."

When he spoke, his voice was gruff. "My parents set the best example for what a marriage is, and they were the best parents a kid could ever wish for. If I can't be the same husband, and dad that my own father was to me and my sister, then I don't have any interest in trying."

She understood, but it didn't mean she agreed with him. To her he just sounded like a wounded person not wanting to admit that one day he'd be whole again.

"Can you stay a little while?" Candace asked as Logan's touch lulled her into a happy, almost asleep state.

He didn't say anything, but he didn't stop touching her, either. She should have turned to him, should have kissed him and enjoyed having a man like Logan in her bed, but she also didn't want to give up the feeling of simply having his arms around her. It had been a long time since she'd trusted someone as much as she trusted this man, and it was something she wanted to selfishly indulge in a little while longer.

"We leave at nine tomorrow morning," Logan murmured in her ear. "I'll be gone when you wake up, but I can either come back and collect you, or you can make your own way to the airport."

Candace was barely conscious she was so relaxed. "There," she murmured. "I'll meet you there."

She tried to stay awake, but as she was slipping into sleep she decided not to fight it. For all she knew, it might be the only time she was cuddled to sleep for a long time.

Candace woke with such a fright it was like a bolt of lightning had struck her. It took a moment, a split second as she struggled to remember where she was and figure out what on earth was happening, but when she did the panic was like a noose around her neck.

"Logan!" she gasped, trying to push herself up.

He was calling out, tossing and turning, the pain and desperation in his voice almost unbearable.

"Logan!" she called out, scrambling from the bed and landing on her feet.

One second Logan was thrashing, the next he was sitting up, looking disorientated, his hands above his head.

"Candace?" Logan's voice was rough, croaky.

She didn't say anything for a moment, just tried to catch her breath.

"Candace?" His voice was more panicked this time.

"Here," she said, leaning forward. "Logan, I'm right here."

He reached to flick the bedside lamp, illuminating the room so she could see him properly and him her.

"What happened?" he asked.

Candace took a big, shaky breath, before sitting on the edge of the bed.

"You were having one of your night terrors and I woke you."

Logan's expression changed, his face falling. "I'm sorry. I don't know what happened."

She reached for him, clasping his hand. "I think you might have these more than you realize," Candace told him, trying to be as gentle with her words and her touch as she could. "Logan, you, well, the other night when I left, it wasn't because I knew about the photos."

He pushed his legs off the bed, head falling into his hands as he sat there. Candace wanted to comfort him, but she also knew that talking about this probably wasn't something he was comfortable with. Wasn't something that would come easily to him.

"I've done this before with you?" he asked when he finally raised his head.

"The other night I woke to you thrashing around and I know I should have done something, but instead I just left," she told him. "I thought maybe it was a one-off thing, and I also didn't think I was going to see you again."

Logan stood, his body dominating the room with his size. "I don't know what to say. I shouldn't have fallen asleep, and I just, I mean…" His voice trailed off, like he was in pain. "I didn't realize that I ever lashed out when I was dreaming. If I'd known I would never have put you in danger like that."

"It's not your fault, Logan. And I'm here for you," she said, even if she *was* scared of it happening again. "I can help."

"Candace," he started, walking around the bed and dropping to his knees as she sat on the bed, reaching for her hands before gently touching her face and then dropping his head into her lap. "I'm sorry."

Tears flooded Candace's eyes, spilled over even as she tried her hardest to push them away. This man—this strong, big man—was literally on his knees before her, and it almost broke her heart.

"It's okay, Logan. Everything's going to be okay."

When he raised his head, she could see that his own cheeks were tearstained. He slowly rose to his feet, and she could hardly breathe, couldn't take her eyes from his face.

"I have to go," he said.

She shook her head but he just nodded, walking backward.

"You can stay," she whispered.

"No, Candace, I need to go. To think. I'm sorry."

Candace watched him leave then lay back on the bed and pulled the covers up, dragging them over her head and hiding away from the world. A part of her wanted to run after him, to grab him and tell him that he couldn't go, but she also knew that he wasn't the kind of man to be forced into anything. If he needed time, he needed time. End of story. He was a complicated guy and she understood that more than he probably realized.

If you love someone, you always need to be strong enough to let them fly.

It was a saying her mom had strongly believed in, and when she shut her eyes, she could hear her saying it, whispering it to her one night when she was a little girl. Then, it had been about her beloved dog, loving him enough to say goodbye the next day at the vet clinic. Now, it was about a man. The only difference was that this time, she wasn't ready to admit how she felt. Not yet.

Logan slammed his fist into his steering wheel so hard that the horn beeped loudly into the otherwise silent night.

All this time thinking no one knew about how much he struggled, about the memories that terrorized him, and there he'd gone and lost it in front of Candace. The fact that she'd seen him…it hurt. Because he'd always been so good at making people see what he wanted them to see, without admitting how hard it had been, coming back from war and losing his parents. Even Brett didn't know the full extent of what he went through every single day—the memories he lived with.

He reached for his dog and stamped out the thoughts that were trying to take over his mind once again, wishing there was something he could do to make them stop. When he was with Candace, his mind actually felt calm, which was why he'd never thought about how he might react in his sleep when he was beside her.

But he'd blown it now. There was no chance she'd turn up in the morning. He'd sealed his own fate there, so now he just had to live with the fact that his past was part of his future, whether he liked it or not. He'd tried to run away from it, and he'd found someone who made him forget, and it still hadn't worked.

Logan started the engine and pulled away, from the hotel and from Candace.

CHAPTER EIGHT

LOGAN TAPPED HIS thigh to tell Ranger to walk at heel, his bag slung over his back, heading for the plane. He'd hardly had any sleep last night, had lain awake thinking about Candace, about his night terrors...*everything*. But he still wanted to head home, and he wasn't so weary that he couldn't make the relatively short flight. Every time he got into the pilot's seat he remembered things he didn't want to recall, but each time he was also pleased that he hadn't given into his fears and stayed grounded. And if he was ever going to get himself together, he needed to keep facing his fears head-on.

He stopped and looked at the plane, prepped and ready for him to fly out in, and his hand fell to Ranger's head.

"Time to head home, buddy," he muttered.

"Logan!"

Logan stopped moving. He'd just presumed Candace wouldn't show, that whatever they had was over after what had happened, but...

"Logan!"

He spun around, not wanting to believe it was her until he could actually see her.

"Candace?" He murmured her name, eyes locking on her as she ran in his direction, her blond curls loose and flying out around her.

She had someone struggling to keep up with her, beside her, and Logan was pretty certain that it was probably a poor security guard who she'd managed to slip past.

"Sorry, Mr. Murdoch. She just..."

"It's fine," he said, once they'd reached him. "It's fine. Sorry for the inconvenience."

"You said nine," Candace panted, out of breath. "It's only one minute past and you'd already given up on me? Surely you know me better than that."

Logan shook his head, speechless. "I didn't expect..."

"You didn't expect me to turn up, did you?" she asked, finishing his sentence. "You thought a little scary dream was going to send me running for the hills?"

He shook his head. "I guess not."

"When we first met, you brazenly asked me out, and I did the one thing in the world I would never usually do," she said. "And that was say yes to you."

Logan stared at her, unable to take his gaze off her bright blue eyes—eyes that had only the night before been filled with tears and were now full of light.

"You pushed me out of my comfort zone, and if you hadn't done that, who knows how long I would have kept on going, stuck in the rut I was in."

"I still don't understand why you're here," Logan

said. Candace could be anywhere in the world right now, and she was waiting to board his plane with him?

"I'm here because the time I've spent with you has been amazing, and because I want to see exactly what this property of yours is like."

He relaxed as she reached for his hand, felt as if all the stress, all the fury that had been building since he'd left her, had just fallen away.

"I'm still invited back to your ranch, aren't I?" Candace asked in a quiet voice.

Logan bent down to kiss Candace's cheek, wishing he could come up with something better to say than simply *yes*.

"I was a jerk last night, Candace, and if I could take it all back, I would."

"You're human, and the thing is that humans make mistakes. Let's just move on from all that, okay?"

Logan nodded, drawing her in close so he could hold her in his arms, feel her soft, warm body against his. It was all he'd thought about as he'd lay alone in his bed, wishing she was still pressed back into him, letting him spoon her.

"Thank you," he whispered.

"There's just one thing," Candace said, hand to his chest as she leaned back and looked up at him.

Logan raised his eyebrows. "What's that?"

"I left a heap of luggage inside the terminal there. Would you be a darling and go grab it all for me?"

Logan burst out laughing and pulled her tight against him for another hug. Talk about surprising a guy in more ways than one.

"I'll get you and Ranger on the plane first, then I'll go back in," he muttered. "But you do realize that there's only so much weight a light aircraft can carry, right?"

She glanced over at his shoulder bag, forlorn on the tarmac, and he followed her gaze.

"Lucky you travel so light then, huh?"

Logan gave her a play punch on the arm and indicated for Ranger to walk with them, wanting her safely seated before he left her.

"I hope you're not this bossy once we get there."

Candace took his hand, her palm swallowed up by his when he closed his over hers. Next time he had the chance to open up to her, he was going to have to man up and deal with it instead of walking away. Because Candace deserved more, and if he was honest with himself, so did he. The fact that she'd turned up was a miracle, and it wasn't one that he was going to take lightly.

Candace took a deep breath as they started their descent. It had only taken a short time, and part of her wished they could have stayed up in the air longer. The view had been incredible the entire way, the day clear and fine, and flying across the Outback had been incredible. When she'd watched the movie *Australia* she'd thought the scenery had been manipulated to make it look so incredible, but she'd even seen kangaroos as they'd flown lower across the Murdoch property, hopping around freely in a way she wouldn't have been able to even imagine had she not seen it with her own eyes.

"You don't really eat kangaroos here, do you?" Candace asked, staring out the window, unable to look away.

"I don't personally, but yeah, a lot of restaurants here serve the meat now."

An involuntary shudder slid down her spine. "That's gross. I can't believe anyone would want to kill such a beautiful animal."

"It's even worse when you find a kangaroo shot by a hunter, or hit by a car, and there's a little joey alive in her pouch."

That made Candace snatch her eyes away from the view. "No."

Logan nodded, but his gaze and concentration never strayed from what he was doing. "Sad but true. When I was a kid I rescued one and she was like a pet for years. We pulled her out of her dead mother's pouch and she ended up being like one of our dogs."

Candace looked back out the window as they fast approached the ground. Logan sure had a way of surprising her.

"This should be nice and smooth, just a little bump when we first touch down," he told her.

Candace glanced over her shoulder at Ranger, sitting alert, his body braced by a harness that was keeping him secure and in place.

"Your dog is incredible. I can't believe he's so well behaved," she said, holding on as they landed and eventually came to a stop.

She watched as Logan flicked switches, looking completely at ease with what he was doing.

"The dogs that make it through SAS training have to be super canines," he said, stretching his arms out above his head. "Ranger had to be completely fearless, whether we were on patrol or being helicoptered into a situation. Sometimes he would be harnessed to my back if we weren't able to land, and we'd parachute to the ground together."

"No way!" It didn't even sound possible that a dog could do that kind of stuff.

"Yes," Logan said with a laugh. "I know it's crazy, but the dogs are probably worth more to the army than we humans are, because at the end of the day there are plenty of guys out there capable of doing our job, with the right training, but not many dogs who could make the cut."

Logan went back to unclip Ranger, and then he was opening his door and disappearing. The next thing, her door opened and he helped her down to the ground.

"You know, I'm almost starting to like dogs because of him," Candace said, stretching and looking around. Her eyes landed on two horses in a nearby field, their ears pricked, bodies dead still as they watched the plane and what was happening. "But I love horses *way* more."

Logan reappeared with some of her luggage, and nodded toward the house. It was a decent walk away, and she felt almost bad for having so much stuff.

"I'll take this lot and the butler can come get the rest."

"You have a butler?" she asked, rushing to catch up to him.

The look Logan gave her made them both laugh.

"Okay, I really fell for that one. But surely you have a trailer or something?"

He bumped his body against hers. "Don't sweat it. I'll come back with the quad bike later."

Ranger ran off ahead and Candace was almost as eager, desperate to see the house that was obviously so special to Logan. She knew it was a big deal him asking her here in the first place, and if she was honest with herself, *not* turning up had never really been an option. Logan had probably been beyond embarrassed about what had happened the night before, and she didn't want him to think he had to deal with his troubles alone.

"So who lives here when you're not around?" she asked.

"We have a manager in a separate house, and his wife keeps the place tidy for me, stocks the fridge when she knows I'm coming back, that sort of thing."

They crossed over toward the house and Candace couldn't help but smile. "It's beautiful."

He was silent for a moment as they walked up to it. "Yeah, it is."

She imagined it still looked the same as it had when his parents had been in residence. It was built from timber with a wide veranda that stretched around the entire house, the almost white paintwork in immaculate condition. As they stepped up toward the front door, Candace touched the handrail and let her hand stay on it until they reached the veranda.

"I can't believe how beautiful this house is. I never realized it would be like this."

Logan moved past her and opened the door.

"You don't keep it locked?" she asked as she followed him inside.

"This is the Outback, not the city. We're miles from our closest neighbor and there's not really any risk of a break-in."

When he put it like that she guessed it made sense—it just wasn't something she was used to.

"So what's the plan for today?" Candace asked. "Horseback riding, a picnic, a swim in some amazing water hole?"

Logan chuckled and set her bags down in the hall. "I actually want to show you something. I was think-ing we'd take a horseback ride there, if you're keen."

Was she keen? "I've been dying to get back in the saddle for months. Just give me a quiet horse, though, because it's been a while."

"That I can do," he said. "Now follow me while I give you a quick tour of the place."

Candace grinned and followed him, happy to look through the house. Taking the high road, and a risk, had been worth it, because she felt like the girl she'd left be-hind before her first album had launched, and she'd been missing that girl a lot lately. She just wanted to have fun, enjoy her life. It wasn't that she wanted to walk away from her career, because she could never stop singing, but creating a sense of balance was something she was determined to achieve.

"These are your parents?" she asked as they passed the hallstand.

Logan stopped, the smile that had been on his face dying. He touched the edge of one of the frames. "Yeah, that's them."

"Well, they look lovely," she said, touching his arm. "It's such a shame I couldn't have met them."

"My mom would have been in a huge flap if I'd brought you here when she was still alive. She'd have been baking up a storm and sending Dad to work in the garden, ordering him around like the queen was about to visit."

Candace liked the mental picture, had a feeling that she'd have probably loved his parents, too. Because that sounded a lot like her grandparents and her mom—just nice people who genuinely cared about their kids.

"So which room am I staying in?" she asked as Logan started to move again.

"That depends if you want to sleep in my bedroom or a guest room," he said, giving her a cheeky wink over his shoulder.

"Let's just see what happens today, shall we? I don't want you getting too cocky, soldier."

She was also a little scared of him having another one of his episodes, but she wasn't going to admit it, not to Logan. *And not one hundred percent to herself, either.*

"So what is it you want to show me?" Candace asked, loving the feel of the sun beating down on her shoulders and the gentle sway of the horse beneath her.

"We're almost there," he replied.

She admired Logan's strong silhouette as he rode slightly ahead of her, his big chestnut gelding tall and well muscled, just like his rider. Where she came from, men were always in the saddle, and it always made her laugh when city folk talked about horseback riding like it was a girls-only sport. Nothing made her admire a man more than one who could ride well and knew how to treat animals.

"Logan, I've been wanting to say that if you'd like to talk about what happened last night, I'm all ears," she said, wanting to get it off her chest to clear the air now rather than have it come up later.

"Can we just wait a minute?" he asked, his face not giving any hint of what he was thinking or feeling. "It'll all kind of make sense soon."

Candace didn't push the point, just accepted it and enjoyed the different scenery as they rode. Everything was so different to what she was used to, but the cattle grazing as they passed had the strange effect of making her feel like she was closer to home than she had been in a long while, even though she was on the other side of the world.

"It's in here," Logan said, heading toward a large shed.

She followed him and dismounted when he did, leading her horse closer and dropping her reins like he did. It wasn't something she was used to doing, but the horses seemed to understand exactly what was required of them.

"They won't move," Logan told her. "Come with me."

He bent down to put a key into the padlock that was securing the door, and she bit her tongue instead of asking why he locked this door in the middle of nowhere yet didn't bother with the house. She could see how tense his body was, that what she was about to see was something that meant a lot to him.

"Logan, what's in here?" she asked, curious and worried at the same time.

He yanked the door open and secured it back so that light flooded the big barn. Candace took a step inside, then another when Logan walked ahead of her. She watched as he dropped to his haunches, before looking back at all the metal and parts in front of her. It took her a second to figure it all out, but then she realized what she was looking at, what the wreckage had once been.

"This was a plane?"

She was staring at the back of Logan's head, waiting for him to explain.

"All my life, flying has been like second nature to me," Logan said, not moving. "I was up in a plane with my dad as soon as I was old enough to tag along, and I got my pilot's license as soon as I was old enough."

Candace swallowed, trying not to hold her breath as she listened to Logan. The way he was talking, the fact that they were standing in front of a wreckage, told her that this story wasn't going to end well. That what he was about to tell her was going to be hard to hear and even harder for him to say.

"Logan, what is this I'm looking at?" she asked.

"My parents died when the plane they were in crashed. My father had clocked up more hours flying than anyone I've ever met before, but the thing he loved killed him and my mom."

"Oh, Logan." Candace blinked away the tears in her

eyes and moved to stand behind him. "I don't know what to say."

"I'd just arrived back into the country when it happened, and even though they were supposed to notify next of kin first, the media got wind of who it was and I saw it on the news before my sister had a chance to phone me."

Now Candace *was* holding her breath.

"I dealt with the accident the only way I knew how, and that started with me insisting that I identify the bodies."

She listened as he sucked back a big breath before continuing on.

"They were badly burned, so…"

Candace put her arms around his waist and pressed herself to his back, just wanting to touch him, to hold him and let him know that she got how hard it was for him to talk, to share what he'd been through. That she was there for him.

"You had all the parts salvaged, didn't you?" she murmured against him.

"My training just kind of kicked in and I insisted on a second, independent investigation once the police one ended inconclusively. I just couldn't understand how a man like my father could be killed doing something he was capable of doing with his eyes shut. Nothing about it seemed right to me."

"Did they find anything?"

"Yeah, but it still doesn't stop me questioning everything, scouring through the report and then coming in here to go over every piece of the plane myself whenever I come home."

She released him enough that she could stand beside him, her arms still around his waist, head tucked against him.

"Yeah, but we can only deal with things the best way we know how."

"When I dream, the terrors I have at night, it's their bodies I see," he told her.

She moved around his body and watched as he shut his eyes, wished she could take away even a little of the pain he was feeling.

"I see them flying, then crashing, watch as they burn alive, and there's nothing I can do to help them. Then suddenly they disappear, and it's my friend Sam I see, being blown to pieces in front of me, his body burning and then somehow ending up alongside my folks, so they're all dead together."

"Have you talked to anyone about this before?" she asked. "Someone who could help you deal with what you're going through?"

Logan shook his head and gazed down at her. "You're the only person I've let close, the only person who's outright asked me about my dreams, and the only person I've ever opened up to about it." He paused. "But I don't want to talk about it anymore, Candace. I want to leave this in the past."

Logan hoped he'd done the right thing, but after so long carrying his pain on his own, it was almost a relief to finally get it off his chest. To show someone the barn he'd kept locked for so long, to talk about his memories. Because he couldn't hide his night terrors from Candace, not after she'd witnessed it firsthand, and he couldn't pretend like they didn't happen any longer, either.

"I don't know what to say, Logan, but I'm pleased you told me."

"It's been a long time since I've felt at peace with the world, but when I'm with you, I don't know. I just feel different."

"Me, too," she said, standing on tiptoe and kissing him. "This isn't something you need to deal with alone, and if you want to talk about your parents all night or not at all, it's fine by me."

Logan had a better idea. It was time he closed this chapter of his life, shut the doors to the wreckage and walked away from trying to find answers that didn't even seem to exist.

"You know, every time I fly my plane, I think about my dad up there in the sky, and I hope he didn't even know what happened when they crashed," Logan admitted, walking hand in hand with Candace from the barn and only dropping the contact to shut the door. "I get a bout of nerves every time I start the engine, but then that passes and I can hear his voice in my head, talking me through every step of the process."

Once he'd locked the door, he turned to find Candace standing as still as a statue, just staring at him.

"You okay?" he asked, forgetting his memories and suddenly worried about her instead.

"I'm fine. Better than fine."

"You know, when I'm with you, everything else just seems to fade away."

"Yeah, for me, too," she whispered in reply, tilting her head back so Logan had to kiss her, so that he couldn't think about anything else. "Everything else just seems to disappear."

"I can't make you any promises, Candace," he whispered, looking down at her. "I would never hurt you, and there is nothing more I want from you than just you, but I'm not..."

"Shhh," she murmured. "Just stop talking and let's forget. Everything."

Logan fell to his knees so he was directly in front of Candace, pulling her down then pushing her back gently until she yielded. He had one hand at her back to guide her down, cushioning her fall as she lay on the grass, rising so he was propped above her.

That was something he could do, something he *wanted* to do. He only hoped that she didn't expect more from him than he could give.

CHAPTER NINE

CANDACE STRETCHED AND pulled herself closer to Logan. She couldn't get enough of him—not his body, not his hands on her, not the feel of being cocooned against him. And now here they were, with hardly any clothes on, lying out under the hot Australian sun.

"We really need to cover up, otherwise we're going to fry like crisps," Logan said, but without making any attempt to move.

"But it feels so good," she murmured, shutting her eyes and basking in the warmth. "Just a bit longer."

"Candace, I don't want to ruin the moment, but I have this feeling that we're setting ourselves up for a fall."

She sighed, putting one hand flat to his chest and using it to prop herself up.

"Can't we just enjoy ourselves and pretend like everything's, I don't know, all going to work out."

Logan smiled up at her, and she leaned down to kiss him, loving the soft fullness of his mouth against hers.

"We can pretend so long as we both know that this is just a short-term thing."

"I know," she said, even though she was still trying to convince herself that she would see Logan again, that somehow they might be able to make something work. "I guess it's just nice to believe that things happen for a reason sometimes, that everything will work out for the best, in the end."

"This did happen for a reason," he told her, stroking a hand up and down her back. "You changed things that had been bothering you for a long time, and I finally showed someone what I've had hidden here. Opened up about what I've been going through."

A low bark made Candace jump. She looked over her shoulder and saw Ranger standing there, a stick dropped at his paws, and a curious look on his face.

"Is it weird that I feel funny about your dog staring at me when I'm practically naked?"

Logan sat up, reaching over for the stick and throwing it. "Yeah, that's definitely weird."

Candace play punched his arm but he just grabbed hold of her, a devilish look on his face.

"This is really bad timing, especially given the whole pretending we're in a bubble conversation we just had, but I had a message early this morning from my old commanding officer, and I have to fly out in a couple of days and head to base. After that, I'll receive my official discharge papers."

Candace shouldn't have expected more, had told herself time and again that this was just a temporary thing, something fun, with Logan. But knowing they only had a couple of days together still hurt.

"I guess I need to book my flight back to the U.S. then," she said, trying to keep her voice upbeat.

"Candace, if there was any way I could just hide out here for the next week, even the next month with you, I would," Logan told her, brushing her hair from her face. "If you want to stay here on your own for a little bit, I'll come straight back once I'm done with work. If you need a vacation where no one will find you, this place is perfect and you'll always be welcome here."

"I can't do that," she murmured, wishing as she said it that she'd just kept her mouth shut and nodded. "The longer I put off seeing my attorney back home and figuring out my management, the worse it'll all be. I've been too good at avoiding things for way too long and I need to head back and deal with it, no matter how good an extended vacation here sounds."

She leaned into Logan's touch, like a cat desperate to be petted.

"If we'd only met in another lifetime, or maybe in a few years..." Logan said.

Didn't she know it?

"You know, we're not so different, you and I," she said.

Logan laughed. "Yeah, except for the fact that I'm a soldier and you're famous."

She touched his cheek with her fingertips. "You might be a soldier, but you're also a ranch owner, and a kind, decent man. There's a lot about your family and your wealth that I think you've kept from me. And besides, I'm just a singer who got lucky. At heart I'm still just a country girl with a big voice, and in my mind that's who I'll always be."

Candace touched her forehead to his, eyes shut because she couldn't bear to look into his eyes.

"But we still come from different worlds. I love the Outback and I've waited my whole life to come back here, and you have a life in America," he told her in a quiet voice. "Even if we weren't so different, we still couldn't ever make this work. Believe me, I've thought it through. Too many times to count."

Hope ignited within her, a gentle tickle that turned into a full-on flip inside her stomach. *He'd actually thought about it?* Even if it was a lost cause, she still liked the fact that he cared enough to think about them being together. She knew it was impossible, that they lived on opposite sides of the world and couldn't possibly make anything long-term work between them, but it wasn't like she hadn't spent time wondering.

"So I guess we just enjoy the next two days and then part ways," she said, needing to say it out aloud to truly get her head around it.

Logan squeezed her hand. "For the record, I've been more content being with you than I've been, well, in forever."

Candace refused to become emotional, because they were both adults making an adult decision. She'd been with men who couldn't tell the truth, and she knew exactly what it was like to be lied to, so the fact that Logan was being honest and open with her wasn't something to mourn. He'd set the bar high for any other men she might meet in the future, and for that she needed to be thankful.

"Can I ask you one question before we stop talking about how little time we have together?"

Logan nodded. "Shoot."

Candace took a shallow breath and blew it straight back out again. "If we did live in the same country, if things were different, would you want to be with me? As in, in a relationship?"

She couldn't believe she'd even asked him that, but she had and she didn't regret it. She needed to know.

"Hell, yes," he whispered straight into her ear. "I can tell you, hand on my heart, that you're the only woman I've ever wanted to open up to. You're special, Candace, and don't let anyone ever make you think differently."

It was all she needed to hear. All the pain of past relationships, of men treating her like a free ticket to a life they wanted, it all just washed away. Because Logan was different, and she needed to make the most of every second in his company.

"Have I mentioned that my all-time favorite movie is *The Bodyguard?*"

Logan smiled as she looped her arms around his neck. "Any scenes you want to reenact?" he asked.

"Oh, there're plenty," she told him, pushing him down so she could straddle him. "In fact, we could role-play *those* scenes all day."

"I wasn't ever very good at drama at school, but I'm a pretty fast learner these days."

She laughed. "Then get ready to play my fantasy role."

And then all at once Logan had her arms pinned at her sides, mouth hot and wet against her skin. Maybe they could role-play later, because this wasn't something she had any intention of putting an end to.

Logan hadn't been so happy in years. Having Candace at home with him, on the property that was more special to him than any other place in the world, had been the best thing he'd ever done. It might only be temporary, but it had at least showed him that maybe he wasn't as screwed up as he'd thought. Damaged, sure, but maybe not beyond repair as he'd thought, *believed,* for so long.

"So what do you say to a walk down memory lane with me?" Logan asked as they rode back to the house, side by side.

Candace gave him a lazy look, like she was ready to fall asleep. Or maybe she was just feeling as relaxed and chilled out as he was.

"What do you have in mind?"

He chuckled to himself as he thought about what they could do, where he could take her. It had been a while since he'd just enjoyed the land he'd grown up on, reminded himself of why he liked the Outback so much. Wherever he'd been in the world, no matter how much pain he'd been in or how bad he'd struggled, this was the place he visualized.

"When we were kids, my sister and I used to ride bareback to a deep water hole, tether the horses and swim. Then we'd eat the lunch Mom had packed us and chill out in the shade for a while."

"Sounds like fun," she said, "although maybe we should stay out of the sun for the rest of the day and do it tomorrow."

"Deal," he agreed. He was more than ready to put his feet up and just chill for the rest of the afternoon and evening. "We can have a barbecue tonight and sit out on the veranda for a while. Listen to the wildlife."

Candace rode a little closer to him. "Speaking of wildlife, there aren't any crocodiles in that water hole, are there?"

He laughed. "We're in New South Wales, sweetheart. It's way too cold down here for crocs."

"Well good," she said. "The last thing I need to worry about is my leg being bitten off."

Logan chuckled and nudged his horse on when she tried to slow down and nibble some long grass. Candace had asked him before whether he'd want to be with her, whether they could have made things work if she lived in Australia or he in America, and he'd told her the truth. Maybe he wouldn't have been so open if there actually *had* been a chance of things working between them, but there wasn't, and he hadn't seen the point in not being honest with her.

Candace had been the breath of fresh air he'd been waiting for, and thinking of never seeing her again wasn't something he wanted to dwell on. All he cared about right now was making sure they made the most of the less than forty-eight hours they had together.

Because after that, she'd just be a memory that kept him going when things got tough.

The water was colder than she'd expected, but the feeling of swinging off an old tire that was attached to a tree overhanging the water hole was worth the initial shock factor.

"Ready to go again?"

Logan's enthusiasm was rubbing off on her, the smile on his face impossible to ignore.

"You're loving this whole feeling of being a kid again, aren't you?" she teased.

He responded by pulling her back farther than he had before, letting go so she flew out over the water. Candace screamed as she let go and landed with a plop, going completely under before emerging. She moved out of the way so Logan could do the same, launching like a missile into the deepest spot, his enthusiasm contagious.

"I can't believe how much fun this is," he said. "It's been years since I've even been down here."

She giggled. "My fans would be horrified that I'm such a kid at heart, but yeah, it's pretty cool."

Logan swam to her, blinking away the water that had caught on his lashes, his short hair looking even darker as it slicked back off his head.

"Would they be horrified about this?" he asked, clasping the back of her head and dragging her body hard to his.

Candace wrapped her legs around him, and her arms, making him tread water to keep them both afloat. "Oh, I think they'd definitely be horrified. Mortified, in fact."

"What about by this?" he asked, flicking the clasp on her bra so that the garment fell forward.

She slid her arms from the straps and watched the bra float away, wrapping her arms around Logan's chest so her bare breasts were against his skin.

"This swimming idea of yours was a pretty good one," she murmured as she kissed him again, nipping his bottom lip when he tried to slide the rest of her underwear off.

She refused to think about leaving, about the short time she had left with Logan, because she hadn't been this happy in years, and there was nothing she could do to stop the clock. All she could do was enjoy being in the arms of a man who was so different to any man she'd ever met before. These memories would last her a lifetime, of that she was certain.

"What say we paddle to shallower water, soldier?" she asked.

Logan tucked her under his arm like he was a lifesaver and headed for shore. "Done."

CHAPTER TEN

"THIS IS A pretty extravagant barbecue," Candace said, smiling up at Logan as he finished ferrying food over to the table.

"I only have one chance to impress you with my grilling, so I wasn't going to take any chances," he told her with a wink.

She laughed as she looked at her plate. "I probably should have made us a salad. You know, so that there was *something* green on our plates."

"What, you don't like my carnivore special?"

Candace looked at the array of meat on her plate and couldn't wipe the grin from her face. He'd done his best to impress her, but she was guessing that aside from grilling meat, he really didn't have any other culinary skills. She slipped Ranger a piece of steak under the table, no longer scared of the big dog's constant presence.

"It's really beautiful here, Logan. I never knew what an amazing country Australia was."

He leaned back in his chair, looking up at the sky. It was almost dark, but Candace could still see his face perfectly. They'd lit candles and placed them on the table, but it wasn't quite dark enough for them to need the extra light.

"It's paradise," he admitted. "Even when I stay here for weeks without leaving, I never stop appreciating how beautiful it is."

Candace wished she could have stayed longer, that she'd just taken Logan up on his offer to stay here while he was away, but she also knew that doing that would be putting off the inevitable.

She looked up at the sky, at the inky blackness peppered with white, and then turned her focus back to Logan.

"What do you say we finish dinner then turn in for an early night?" she asked.

"I think," he said, reaching for her hand across the table, "that you might just be a mind reader."

Candace was finding it hard to fall asleep. She'd snuggled up to Logan after they'd made love, and he'd promptly fallen into a deep slumber, but she couldn't stop thinking about leaving. About the fact that their holiday romance was almost over. Or that at any moment he could have one of his nightmares and end up thrashing around beside her.

She knew that he'd snuck out of bed the night before, because she'd woken to find him gone. He'd slept in another room, and then come back to their shared bed early in the morning. But tonight he'd fallen asleep without probably even meaning to.

Candace tried to shut off the overthinking part of

her brain and closed her eyes, listening to Logan's steady heartbeat beneath her, enjoying the warmth of his body. But just as soon as she'd relaxed, as if on cue, his heart started to race so loud that she could hear it. Before she had time to move, he was yelling out, his arm thrashing, smashing into her face as she tried to roll out of his way.

"No!"

"Logan, wake up!" she screamed, landing on the floor and yanking a blanket with her to cover her naked body.

Ranger was at her side, confused, and she held on to him as Logan leaped up, looking like a wild man in the moonlight spilling in through the windows.

"Candace? Where, what…"

Then he saw her and his shoulders dropped. He looked horrified at what he'd done.

"Sweetheart, I'm sorry," he murmured, walking around the bed and reaching a hand out to her. "I'm so, so sorry."

"Logan, you can say sorry all you like, but you need to do something about this," she murmured, knowing she couldn't just pretend like he was okay, act like everything would be fine just because he'd managed to talk to her about his nightmares. "You need help."

"It won't happen again, I can sleep in a different room, I…" He ran a hand through his hair before walking a step backward and sitting on the bed.

Candace stood up, her body shaking as she lifted a hand to her face, touching gently across her cheek.

"Logan, you hit me," she whispered, her voice cracking with emotion.

He stared at her, raised his hand then let it fall to the bed beside him. "Candace, I…" Logan took a deep breath. "Did I hurt you?"

"Logan, you need to talk to someone. If not me, then a professional, but you can't torture yourself in your dreams like that every night. It has nothing to do with you almost hurting me, and everything to do with you hurting yourself by not getting help. This isn't just going to go away."

"I don't have a problem and I don't want to talk about it. I can deal with this on my own," he growled out. "And for the record, what happened just now has everything to do with me almost hurting you. I don't care about me, but I *sure as hell do* care about what I could have done to you."

Candace closed her eyes for a beat. "Yeah, I think you do have a problem, Logan. One that could be fixed if you weren't so scared about facing your past."

He stood up, hands clenched at his sides. "This was a mistake. We don't even know each other and now you're trying to tell me…you know what, I think we're done here, Candace. I am who I am, and I can't change that."

Candace was done with being patient, because Logan was being a bullheaded macho male now, and she wasn't going to let him get away with it. She didn't care if she'd had a fantastic time with him—they also had to deal with reality. Maybe she'd been right to doubt her ability to make a judgment call when it came to men.

"I think you're right," she said, jutting her chin up and wishing she was taller. "Whatever this was, it's over."

Logan stood and stared at her, like he was going to reach for her, going to say something that would turn the entire situation around. She waited, never even blinking as she watched him for fear of crying, but in the end, he turned and walked out of the room.

"I think we should leave tomorrow," she said, willing her voice not to crack.

"Yeah, first thing in the morning."

She watched Logan go and didn't falter until he shut the door behind him. Then she collapsed onto the bed, face buried in the pillow and sobbed like she'd never cried before in her lifetime.

After so long protecting her heart, not letting anyone get too close to her, Logan had snuck past her defenses and managed to hurt her when she'd least expected it. When she'd thought there was nothing he could do to wound her. She should never have let herself be put in this situation, should have protected her heart instead of being vulnerable to Logan. Letting him get closer to her had been a stupid thing to do, and she should have known better.

Either way, there was nothing she could do to stop the pain shooting through her body like a drug being pumped through her veins. Whatever she'd had with Logan, it was over, and no matter what she tried to tell herself, dealing with never seeing him again was…

She swallowed the emotion that choked in her throat,

refusing to let it sink its claws in to take hold. But the pain was too much, the ache in her heart...

Unbearable.

Logan slammed his palm down onto the kitchen counter and hung his head. He was a total idiot. A bloody fool. And because he was incapable of dealing with his problems, he'd just walked away from the one woman he could have just been himself around. Who didn't care who he was, what his family name was, or what he'd been through. The one person who had simply been trying to help him.

Candace had given him a chance to open up and be himself, to acknowledge the nightmares that woke him almost every night, that haunted him, and instead he'd walked out on her and as good as told her it was over. All because she'd been brave enough to confront him, to try to get him to admit that he needed help.

Logan slumped forward, exhausted and unsure what he was supposed to do next. He should have turned around and walked straight back into his bedroom, begged for her forgiveness and just admitted he needed professional help, but his pride or some other stupid emotion was stopping him. He'd never acknowledged what he went through every night to anyone other than Candace, and talking to anyone else, dealing with it properly, wasn't something he was ready for.

He'd told Candace so much, had admitted so much to her that he'd hardly ever spoken to anyone else about, and yet when it came to admitting his shortfalls, acknowledging his true weakness...

Logan sat back, took a deep breath and straightened his body. The best thing for both of them was for this to end now, to stop things before they went any further when they both knew there was no future for them as a couple anyway. The whole idea of bringing her here with him had been stupid. Ridiculous even.

If that was true, though, then why did ending things with Candace seem like the stupidest thing he'd ever done in his life?

CHAPTER ELEVEN

"So I GUESS this is it, then?"

They'd both been silent on the journey back to Sydney, and now they were standing outside the plane, Candace's luggage sitting on the tarmac. Logan had Ranger on his leash, at his side, and he'd asked someone to come and get all of Candace's things. Which gave them about another five minutes together.

"I'm sorry things had to end this way," Candace said, not taking her sunglasses off.

Logan didn't hesitate—he stepped forward, took her handbag and put it down, before wrapping her in a tight hug. He shut his eyes as she tucked into him, snuggled to his chest, her arms holding him just as tight around his waist. She probably hated him for what had happened, but he wasn't going to let her get on that plane without at least trying to show her what she'd come to mean to him.

"I'll never forget you, Logan. No matter what," she whispered, just loud enough for him to hear.

Logan kissed the top of her head, before putting his hands on her arms to hold her back. Her eyes were swimming with tears when he pushed her sunglasses to the top of her head, and if he wasn't fighting it so hard, his would be, too. All the times he managed to stamp out his emotions on tour, and here he was about to cry. Because this was about more than saying good-bye; this was about him being forced to deal with his past, with his terrors.

"One day, when you're old and gray, surrounded by ten grandchildren, you can smile and think about the naughty Australian vacation you had when you were a young woman," he told her, staring into her blue eyes. "Just promise me that you'll always remember me with a smile, because that's how I'll remember you, even if things didn't work out as, well, you know."

Candace shook her head, like she was trying to shake away her emotion.

Logan bent down to kiss her cheek, tasting the salti-ness of her tears as she let him touch her skin.

"Goodbye," she said when she broke away.

Her bags were being loaded onto a cart behind them, and he knew it was time for her to go. They should never have even crossed paths in the first place, which meant they'd always been on borrowed time, and after the way things had gone last night, he was lucky she was even talking to him right now.

Logan watched as she gave Ranger a hug before straightening.

"You, my boy, are very special, you know that? I think I might just like dogs now that I've met you."

"Goodbye," Logan said as she walked away.

Logan waved then thrust his hands into his jeans'

pockets, eyes never leaving her as she turned and walked away. Candace was gone, and it was time for him to get on a plane himself and close the final chapter of his life as a SAS soldier. And maybe, just maybe, he'd think about what she'd said to him.

It was goodbye to the job he'd loved, and the woman he could so easily have fallen in love with, all in one day. Time to move on. Pity it wasn't as easy as it sounded. All he could do now was take his life one day at a time, and figure out what his future held. Because right now he was more confused than he'd ever been, and he also knew he'd been a jerk for not sucking up his pride and admitting his shortfalls to her. Because Candace had been there for him like no other woman probably ever would be.

Candace boarded the plane and smiled at the flight attendant who took her bag and put it in the overhead cabin. She took her seat, pleased she'd purchased both the first class seats that were side by side. The last thing she wanted was someone trying to make small talk with her, and she sure didn't want anyone to see her crying.

But there was something different about Logan, and she knew it. There was nothing she could think about him that would change her mind, and there was nothing she could do to pull herself from the mood she was in. After what had happened during the night, and then actually walking away from him…it was all too much. He'd behaved badly and she didn't regret what she'd said, but it still hurt.

"Would you like a drink before takeoff?"

Candace refused to take her grumpiness out on anyone else, so she forced a smile and nodded. She may as well drink something that would take the edge off her pain, or at the very least knock her out for part of the long trip home.

"Champagne," she said after a moment's hesitation. "Please."

Maybe she needed to celebrate the few days she'd just had, minus their argument. She needed to toast it and then forget it, because in the end Logan wasn't a man she could never have been with. Not when he refused to do something about a problem that was so serious, and not when they lived on opposite sides of the world.

"Here we go, ma'am. A glass of champagne for you."

Candace took the glass, shut her eyes and took a sip. It was heavenly. She had fourteen hours before she touched down at LAX, and a few more glasses were probably exactly what the doctor would order. She could pass out and sleep until the plane landed.

No more tears, no more feeling sorry for herself. She was a woman in charge of her own life now, she'd met a man who'd changed the way she thought about *everything,* and she was going home to start over. When she thought about Logan, she needed to learn how to smile instead of frown, and make the memories of her time with him last forever. She needed to simply remember the *good* times she'd had with him and forget the rest.

Today was the first day of the rest of her life. And if there was one thing Logan had taught her, it was that she had to trust her own instincts and learn to put herself first.

CHAPTER TWELVE

LOGAN STOOD OUTSIDE the plane and stretched. He was exhausted. Not the kind of bone-tired exhaustion that he'd experienced on tour, but he was still ready to collapse into bed and not stir until late the next morning. The smart thing to do would have been to stay in the city for the night, but he'd already let his apartment and his only option would have been to crash at Jamie and Brett's. He doubted any respectable hotel would have let him arrive with Ranger, even if he explained how highly trained he was, and he didn't want Jamie's pity. The way she'd look at him would only remind him of what he'd lost since last time he'd seen her.

"I'm getting old," he muttered to his dog, bending to give him a scratch on the head. "We were definitely ready to retire."

Ranger looked up at him, waiting for a signal that it was okay to run off, and Logan waved him on. He threw his pack over his back and headed for the house. *So much for planning to be gone only a few days, a week at the most*. He'd ended up being talked into spending time with some of the newer recruits in the K9 division, which he was pretty sure was his superior's way of trying to push him into a teaching position. It wasn't that he hadn't enjoyed it—he had, and Ranger had, too—but after so long thinking about coming back home, he was more than ready to make it happen. Not to mention the fact that he wasn't ready to make any long-term commitments just yet.

Logan stopped when he noticed a light on in the house. *Weird.* He hadn't phoned ahead and told the manager he'd be back a day early, which meant they wouldn't have bothered to go and turn lights on, and... *crap.* There was smoke coming from the chimney. Either his manager had decided to take some serious liberties and move into the main house, or there was a squatter or someone in there. His sister was away at a conference, and she was the only other person who had a key, and the right, to enter their house.

He broke into a jog, whistling out to Ranger to come back. His dog was trained to sniff out bombs, but he was also a lethal weapon when it came to providing protection when he had to be. Logan knew he was better with the dog at his side than a weapon, especially if there was an intruder.

He moved quietly up the steps, breathing slowly and filling his lungs as he trod, before trying the door handle. It was unlocked. Logan pushed it open, glanced at his dog and tapped his thigh so he stayed right at his side, and closed it behind them. He listened and heard only the low hum of the television, so he walked silently down the hall, pausing to listen before turning into the kitchen. There was a cup on the counter that he hadn't left there, and a couple of shopping bags sitting on the floor.

Someone had definitely been making themselves at home in his absence, and he wanted to know right now what on earth was going on.

Logan could see the television from where he was standing, saw the closing credits of a movie, but he couldn't hear anything else. He stepped carefully, not wanting to make any of the wooden floorboards creak, hardly breathing as he saw a foot sticking out. That someone was lying on his sofa.

"What the hell…" Logan's voice died in his throat as he leaped around the corner of the sofa.

No. He must be dreaming. Seeing things.

He bent to silence Ranger, still staring at the woman lying, asleep, her lips slightly parted, long blond hair messy and covering the cushions beneath her head and shoulders.

Candace. The woman he'd done nothing but think about these past two weeks was actually in his home, lying on his sofa. Logan had been so close to trying to track her down, but he hadn't even asked for her phone number before they'd parted ways, which he'd been telling himself had been smart, not having any of her contact details.

But now she was here? He couldn't believe it. *He didn't believe it.*

Logan bent to retrieve the television remote, hitting the off button, and disappearing to find a blanket. In his room the bed was slightly crinkled, and when he went to yank the comforter off, a hissing noise startled him. Then Ranger's low growl put him on high alert.

"Leave it," he ordered, wondering what kind of animal had gotten into his room.

A head popped out from between the pillows, followed by a yawn and a stretch. Candace was in his house, and she'd brought her cats with her? Logan pulled the comforter off despite the kitty's protests and put a hand on Ranger's head to settle him. The poor dog looked like his eyes were going to pop out of his head and he didn't blame him. Heck, *his eyes* had just about popped out of his head when he'd seen Candace.

"Easy, boy. It's just a cat. You're still the boss."

Logan returned to the living room, put a few more logs on the fire and stood above Candace, still wondering if he was imagining the whole thing. He was insanely tired, so it wouldn't be impossible for him to be dreaming, but…He reached down to stroke her hair from her face, smiling when she stirred slightly. There was no imagining that. Candace was on his sofa, asleep, and he wasn't going to waste any more time in joining her.

He sat on the edge of the sofa, gently scooped her and moved her across a little, then lay beside her, covering them both with the comforter and wrapping one arm around Candace. The feel of her body, the smell of her perfume, the softness of her hair against his face— they were things he'd tried to commit to memory and been so worried he'd forget.

Logan wanted to lie awake, or even better wake Candace up so he could find out what on earth she was doing back in Australia, but the desire to sleep was too strong to ignore. He relaxed his body into hers and shut his eyes, letting slumber find him. Tomorrow he could ask her all about it. Tonight, he was just going to enjoy having her beside him and falling into the sleep he'd been craving for hours. And after all the therapy he'd gone through, the therapy he'd finally admitted to needing, he was at least confident that he wouldn't hurt her.

Candace had the strangest feeling that she couldn't breathe. In her dream, there was something stuck on her chest, pressing her down, but when she opened her eyes the panicked feeling almost immediately washed away. *Logan.* Light was filtering into the room, so she knew it was early, which meant he must have arrived in the night and found her asleep.

She wriggled to move his arm down, the weight of it across her chest too heavy, and then turned on her side to stare at him. She had no idea what he was going to say or how he was going to react, and the idea of telling him what she'd done absolutely terrified her, but she was going to do it. *Fear was no longer going to stop her from doing what her heart told her was right.*

Candace touched one hand to Logan's cheek, trailing her fingers across his skin. He hadn't shaved for at least a day, so the stubble was rough against her fingertips. It took every inch of her willpower not to trace the outline of his lips, parted and full in slumber. But what was even more amazing was that they'd both slept—he hadn't woken like he had every other time she'd spent the night with him.

"Now that you've woken me, you'd better kiss me," Logan mumbled, eyes still shut.

She smiled, not surprised he'd tricked her and been awake, but she also did as she was told. Candace wriggled closer to him, their bodies intertwined, slowly touching her lips to his in a kiss so sweet it made her sigh. Logan's mouth moved slowly, lazily, against hers, like he was still half asleep, and it suited her fine to start things out slow, to just enjoy being this close to the man she'd thought of constantly since the day she'd left him.

"Now that's what I call a nice way to wake up," he mumbled.

Candace kissed him again, not so gently this time, one hand snaking around his neck and running through his hair as she pulled herself closer to him.

"Mmm, this morning just keeps getting better and better."

She pulled away only to look at him, to see if he'd opened his eyes, and he had.

"Hey," she said, staring into his hazel brown gaze.

"Hey," he said straight back, stretching his legs out and then slinging one over hers.

"Were you surprised to find me here?"

Logan chuckled. "Surprised would be putting it mildly."

She had no idea what he was thinking, but he hadn't exactly been opposed to her kisses, and he *had* cuddled up to her on the sofa while she was sleeping, which told her that he obviously wasn't unhappy to find her.

"I guess I should have called ahead first, huh?"

He raised an eyebrow. "It would have stopped me

from almost having a heart attack and thinking squatters were in my house."

"Sorry," she said, starting to wonder whether she had been crazy to just move in while he was away, without asking him.

"Then again, being exhausted and actually sleeping through an entire night with you by my side was worth the near-death experience."

Candace sat up, wanting to tread lightly with what she was about to say. "Logan, I can't believe you slept the whole night without…"

"Freaking out and having my terrors," he finished for her. "Yeah, it looks like I did."

She lay back down again, this time covering his chest, her cheek flat to his body.

"I can't believe it."

"Well, believe it," he said, rubbing her back. "You've changed me, Candace, in more ways than I'd like to admit. Because I finally got the help I needed."

She listened to him take a deep breath, his expression serious. "The way I reacted the other night when you confronted me," he started.

"Was a knee-jerk reaction to being pushed too hard," she interrupted, the kindness in his eyes making her want to just hold him and never let go. "I should have known that it wasn't something you could be pushed into dealing with."

"But pushing was exactly what I needed," he told her, stroking her cheek. "I was being pigheaded, and I owe you an apology."

"Can I tell you something?" she asked.

"Of course."

"I want to explain why I was so scared of you the other night," she started.

Logan frowned. "Because I understandably scared the crap out of you?"

She gave him a half smile, nestling in closer to him. "No, because the last man I was with, the one I thought was different than the rest because he wasn't interested in my fame or my money, he…"

Logan touched her hair, left his hand there and waited for her to continue.

"He was my husband, Logan, and he hit me, and when I went to leave, to call for help, he grabbed me so tight around the throat that I thought he was going to strangle me."

It was as if all the blood had drained from Logan's face when she glanced up at him.

"So when I struck out at you…"

Candace grabbed his hand and touched his fingers to her cheek. "You didn't even make a bruise here, Logan, but yeah, when I woke up to you going crazy it really scared me. Kind of brought a heap of memories back that I've been trying to forget. It was just all too much, one nightmare too many."

"No wonder we get on so well," he said, refusing to react to what she'd told him, to get angry when there was nothing he could do about what had happened to her. "We're both kind of screwed up about the past, huh?"

"I guess you could say that," she muttered, closing her eyes as he leaned down to kiss her. "I've met a lot of men that seemed so right at the start, but with every relationship that's failed, it's just made it so hard for me to trust in anyone. Because it's not just men who've used me, or tried to, it's been so-called friends, too."

"So you being here?" he asked.

Candace shut her eyes, knowing she needed to tell him what her being here actually meant. That she hadn't just flown in for a few days, that this was a whole lot more permanent than that. *If he'd have her.* That all she'd done since she'd left was think of all the reasons why she shouldn't have lost her temper with Logan, why she needed to take a leaf out of her own book and open up to him, to talk to someone about her past and why it haunted her so badly.

"Logan, I kind of took a risk just turning up like this, but something you said to me, something we talked about, just kept running through my mind after I'd left."

He was watching her intently, waiting for her to continue.

"I'm not just here for another vacation," she admitted.

"I kind of guessed that when I found one of your cats on my bed," Logan told her, his grin telling her that he knew exactly what was going on.

"When you said that if we lived in the same country, if we'd met at a different time or place, that things could have worked out between us…" She paused. "Did you mean it?"

He sighed and stroked her hair. "Of course I meant it."

"So, does the fact that I kind of just moved to Australia mean..." Candace stopped talking, knowing he knew exactly what she was trying to say to him.

Logan sat up, back against the armrest of the sofa. "You mean to say that while I was away working, you flew halfway across the world with your cats in tow to move into my house and surprise me?" He paused. "And forgive me?"

Candace's face flushed, the heat rising up her neck and into her cheeks. "When you put it like that you make me sound like a crazy person."

"You," he said, pulling her against him so she was firm to his chest, "are not a crazy person."

"So you do want me here?" she mumbled.

"Yes, I want you here," Logan said, squeezing her and dropping a kiss into her hair. "You and your crazy cats will always have a home here, Candace. Always."

From the moment she'd walked through the door with all her things, Candace had started to worry. What had seemed like such a great idea back in L.A. had seemed stupid and childish once she'd arrived, but having Logan by her side, seeing the look on his face when he'd woken with her in his arms, had made everything okay. It was the first time she'd ever taken a risk, except for the time her mom had forced a record label executive to listen to her songs, and both times they'd changed her life for the better.

"So now that you're here, are you going to be my barefoot housewife, cooking me three meals a day and tending to my every need?" Logan joked.

Candace laughed. "You wish, soldier. You wish."

Ranger came over and poked his head between them,

looking for some affection, and Candace stopped touching Logan and ran her hand across the dog's fur instead. She couldn't believe that after a lifetime of being scared of large dogs, she'd warmed to Logan's big canine so quickly.

"Poor boy was traumatized by your cats last night," Logan told her.

"Sorry, Ranger," she cooed. "Those mean old cats might try to take over, but you stand firm, okay?"

They sat in silence for a long while, Candace stroking Ranger's head and Logan running his fingers gently through her curls.

"I don't want to ruin the moment, but have you really thought about what it'll be like living here, when you're so used to such a, well, a glamorous lifestyle?" Logan asked. "And just because I've started to get help doesn't mean we aren't going to hit a few road bumps along the way." He paused. "I did dream last night, Candace, but it wasn't as bad and I was able to deal with it. To pull myself out of it somehow and use you to push the memories away and fall back asleep."

Candace's heart started to beat faster.

"So have you really thought this through?" he asked again.

Yes, it was *all* she'd thought about when she was trying to figure out whether moving was a good idea or not, but at the end of the day, she knew that having a partner in life was way more important than anything else. Her success as a recording artist wasn't going to keep her warm in bed at night, or give her someone to confide in and travel with, to start a family with. And the fact that Logan had actually done something about his terrors? That just made her decision seem all the more *right*.

"Logan, I've been performing for eight years now, and even though I love it, I don't think it's enough anymore."

"And you're sure this is what you want, though?" he asked. "Don't get me wrong, I want you here, but I don't want you to look back in a few months, or even a few years, and wish you'd thought it through more."

"I want you," she said, taking her hand off Ranger and pressing it to his cheek, looking up into his eyes. "It might mean a change of pace, but I'm okay with that. I'm *ready* for that. Because I honestly believe that this is where I'm supposed to be."

Logan's eyes crinkled ever so slightly at the corners, his smile making her entire body tingle.

"Why do I feel like you have this all planned out?" he asked.

She laughed. "Well, it just so happens that I've had a lot of time to think this through."

Logan groaned but she kissed him to stop it. He ran his fingers down her back and hoisted her up on top of him, letting her sit on top but taking charge of her mouth.

"Don't you want me to tell you all my great ideas?" she asked, pulling back.

Logan leaned up, cupping the back of her head and forcing her back down, kissing her again.

"No," he mumbled when she fought against him again, laughing. "Just let me enjoy being with you for a while before you map my whole life out for me. Unless, of course, you've written a song about me?"

"Yeah. I called it 'Bodyguard'," she joked.

"Oh, really?"

"Logan!" she protested when he tried to flip her beneath him.

He stopped, rolling to his side and dragging her with him. "Fine, go on then. I can see we're not going to have any fun until you tell me all your plans."

Candace laughed, but he was right—she did have everything all planned out, because planning had been the only way she'd been able to convince herself to take a risk, follow her instincts, and move halfway across the world.

"I figured we could keep a place in town, so we're only a short flight away from the city when we want to head in, but we'd obviously spend most of our downtime here."

"When you say downtime?" he asked.

"I have a tour next year that I can't cancel, so I was thinking that you could be my bodyguard," she said. "You *and* Ranger."

"Oh, you were, were you?" Logan muttered.

"It'll be busy at times, and I'll have to go back to L.A. to record another album at some stage, because I've already signed for one more, but after that we can decide on what works for us both, together. What do you think?"

Logan was trying hard not to laugh. As Candace talked excitedly, she reminded him of a little bright-colored parrot chirping a million miles an hour. It was impossible not to smile just watching her talk so animatedly, but his gaze was constantly drawn to her mouth, those pillowy lips of hers his weakness.

"Logan?"

He switched his gaze back to her eyes. "What was the question?" Logan had no idea what she'd even been talking about at the end there, but whatever she'd said he was inclined to just agree.

"I said does all that sound okay with you? I don't want to sound like I'm trying to organize your life, but it's going to take a bit of juggling at the start."

Logan smiled at the worried expression on her face, trying to reassure her. "Sweetheart, so long as I have you by my side and I get to spend a decent chunk of the year here at home, I'm happy. Everything else we can figure out as we go."

He'd never been more pleased to have his life organized for him, especially now that he was confident he could deal with his past, that he'd received the help he needed. And help was only a phone call away now, so he didn't have to burden Candace with everything when he needed to talk through his night terrors some more.

"You're sure?" she asked, bottom lip caught between her teeth.

"I spent the past couple of weeks in a foul mood even though I promised you I'd think about you and smile," he told her honestly. "I couldn't believe that I'd finally met someone I could actually be with, who I wanted to be with, and I only got such a short time with her. Or that I'd acted like such a jerk when I should have been taking care of her."

Candace seemed to melt into him, her entire body relaxing at hearing his words.

"Really?"

"Really." Logan pushed her up a little and hooked a finger under her chin, tilting her face up so he could look into her eyes. "You're the best thing that has ever happened to me, Candace, and I will do whatever it takes to make this work."

"Me, too," she sighed.

Logan was about to kiss her, but he hovered for a moment. "You do realize that Ranger has to come everywhere with us, though, right? I promised him a retirement by my side, and after what he did for me on the tours we went on, I can't go back on my word."

"Okay, so you *and* your goofy dog."

Logan broke their kiss as soon as he'd started it. "Who you calling goofy? Ranger has..."

"I know how awesome your dog is," Candace said with a laugh. "So just shut up and kiss me, would you?"

Logan didn't need to be asked twice. He kissed Candace slowly, groaning when she raked her fingernails through his hair, forcing himself to take things slowly. Because there was no rush now—they had all day together, and the day after that. *The month after that.*

He might have lost a lot, seen things that he'd never forget and that would haunt him for the rest of his life, but now he had Candace. And for all the darkness of his past, he now had her like a shiny bright light beaming into his future. There was no way he was ever going to let her walk away again, not if he could help it.

"I love you," he whispered as she pulled back, looking up at him.

Candace had tears swimming in her eyes, but her smile told him they were happy tears.

"I love, too, Logan," she whispered back.

Logan shook his head as he pulled her in for another kiss. How he'd managed to end up with Candace Evans in his life, in his heart, he'd never know. But he sure wasn't complaining.

EPILOGUE

"Have I thanked you for being my bridesmaid?"

Jamie laughed, and Candace watched as she filled two spiraled glasses high with champagne.

"If you tell me one more time…"

"Sorry," Candace apologized, taking her glass and taking a nervous sip. "I just still can't believe that it's just the four of us here, that I'm about to get married."

"Stop," Jamie ordered, her hand closing over Candace's forearm. Her grip was light, but her intention was clear. "I don't want to see that panicked look in your eyes again, because I have no desire to chase you down the street if you go all runaway bride on me."

Candace took a deep breath, staring at her slightly shaking hand. "I just find it hard to believe that after so long, after everything, I'm standing here."

"Well, believe it," Jamie said, holding her glass high so they could touch them together. "I never believed that I would ever be with anyone ever again after my first husband died, but sometimes we just have to accept that things happen for a reason. Those men out there waiting for us?"

Candace nudged aside the blinds, searching for Logan. She saw his big silhouette almost immediately, sitting on the beach in just a pair of shorts. His skin was golden, his dark hair damp, off his face like he'd just run his fingers through it. She hoped he wasn't having any last minutes nerves, wasn't trying to devise a plan with Brett to make a run for it.

She pushed those thoughts away. It had been a year since she'd moved to Australia, and not once had Logan given her the impression that he was unhappy. It had been the best twelve months of her life.

"We're pretty lucky, huh?"

Candace blinked away the tears that had filled her eyes, wishing she didn't keep getting so emotional. Everything seemed to set her off these days—just the thought of standing in front of Logan and saying "I do" was enough to make her want to burst out crying.

"I was so lost when I met Logan, and he just took me under his wing like I was a broken bird in need of tender loving care. He healed me, Jamie," Candace said, tears now falling slowly down her cheeks. "I never thought anyone ever could, but he did it like it was the easiest thing in the world."

Jamie plucked a tissue and crossed the room to gently wipe her cheeks. "You know you saved Logan, too, don't you?"

Candace took the tissue and dabbed closer to her eyes and then her nose. "Logan was fine just the way he was. I was the fragile one."

She knew more than anyone else ever would that Logan had been suffering, that he'd been in so much pain from his past, but she also knew how strong he was. There wasn't a doubt in her mind that he'd have found a way to pull through and find happiness.

"No." Jamie shook her head, taking her own look out the window. "Logan has always been so good at hiding how he feels, making us all think he's okay, but the truth is that he's been hurting and alone for a long time. He didn't cope well when Brett and I told him we were together, and I'm not sure he's ever gotten over Sam's death, or what happened to his parents. Add his last tour to the Middle East into the mix?" Jamie sighed, before turning back around and reaching for her champagne flute. "We were worried about him. Until he met you."

Candace blinked away the last of her tears and sipped her drink to take her mind off everything. Deep down she knew that Jamie was right, but she was just so grateful for what Logan had done for her that it was hard to believe she could have done the same for him.

"I think we need to get dressed," she announced, putting her glass down and walking over to the wardrobe.

She opened the door and couldn't help the smile that spread across her face when she saw her dress. It was white, covered in the tiniest white jewels that caught the light like diamonds. Candace had already placed the same jewels in her hair, just a handful of them so they looked like raindrops against her blond curls, which were loose and tumbling around her shoulders.

"I still can't believe that you didn't even bring a makeup artist here," Jamie said with a laugh. "You're used to a whole entourage, and instead you've just got me."

"Well, believe it," Candace said, untying her robe and letting it fall to the floor so she was just standing in her underwear, before stepping into her dress. "The best thing we ever did was decide to come here, just the four of us. Although I'm sure we'll find out that there was a rogue long lens taking snaps of us when we get back."

"I don't care who takes a photo of me, I'm just in shock still that we're here," Jamie replied, zipping up the dress without having to be asked. "I still can't believe we have a butler just for our villa."

"It's Hayman Island, baby," Candace said with a drawl, imitating Logan when they'd first arrived. "Get used to living in the lap of luxury."

"And I will never stop thanking you for as long as I live. Seriously, I know you're used to the rich and famous lifestyle, but for us regular people, this is beyond incredible. It's the vacation of a lifetime for me."

Candace wriggled, getting her dress right, before spinning to look in the full-length mirror.

"Don't mention it. You deserved an amazing vacation, and for the record, I will never get used to coming to places like this. I still have to pinch myself." She sighed. "Besides, what fun would Logan and I have without you two? I foresee plenty of trips in the near future."

"Yes to that!"

Jamie took off her robe and slipped her dress on, and

Candace turned her back slightly to give her privacy until she felt her friend's hand on her arm.

"I think I also owe you thanks for letting me wear something beautiful. Last time I was bridesmaid I think the bride intentionally wanted to make us look terrible in case we stole the show!"

"Well, you do look beautiful," Candace told her, touching up her lip gloss before picking up the single, long-stemmed white tulip that had been resting on the bed.

They linked arms, took one final sip of champagne each, and stared at one another.

"Do you think they'll even be off the beach yet?"

Jamie laughed. "Sweetheart, those boys have spent all their adult lives in the military. There's not even a chance they'll be late to this."

Candace knew it was silly, and they only had to walk out the door and down the beach a little, but part of her was worried that Logan wasn't going to be there, that she'd just dreamed the past few months and reality was going to come crashing down.

"There he is."

Jamie's whispered words made Candace stop walking, clutching her friend's hand tight. She was right; he was there. Standing on the beach, barefoot, linen pants rolled up, wearing a half-buttoned loose white shirt and a smile that made her want to run into his arms.

"Oh, my gosh," she muttered, but the words just came out as one garbled sentence.

"Take a deep breath and just start walking."

Candace did as she was told, eyes locked on Logan's as they walked, even from this distance. She was aware that Brett was standing close to him, that there was a celebrant there, too, but all she could really see was the man she was about to marry. Tears welled in her eyes again, but she forced them back, wanting to bask in the happiness of being on an almost secluded beach, with the three people who'd grown to mean so much to her in only a year.

"I hope he knows how much I love him," she whispered to Jamie, still fighting the urge to run to him in case it *was* all a dream that she was about to wake up from.

"He does," she whispered back, "but tell him again anyway."

Logan took his eyes off Candace for a split second to glance at Brett.

"Do you think she's going to regret this? I mean, look at her."

"Sorry, mate. I only have eyes for the woman walking beside her," Brett said with a laugh. "But yeah, she probably will. I mean, you're just some commoner, right?"

Logan knew he should have waited, that he was supposed to stand with Brett until the girls reached them, but seeing Candace walk toward him was too much. He wanted her by his side, in his arms, and he wanted her now.

Thank God he was her bodyguard and had an excuse to be at her side all the time, because even seeing her walk alone made his protective instincts go into overdrive. He was so used to taking care of her when she was working that he couldn't stand to see her walking on her own.

"Where are you going?" Brett muttered as he left him.

Logan didn't bother answering, he just stared at Candace as he closed the distance between them, only stopping when he had his arms around her and his lips pressed to hers. Today was about telling the world she was his, that he was ready to be with her forever, and he was more than ready to stake his claim.

"Logan!" she exclaimed when he broke their kiss.

"What? I was impatient waiting down there."

He gave her a wink and took her hand, laughing at the eye roll Jamie gave him. Not that she could get away with teasing him after the way she behaved with Brett.

"You look absolutely beautiful, Candace," he told her, raising their hands to drop a kiss to hers. "And you, too, Jamie."

Jamie made a noise in her throat and joined Brett, and Logan kept hold of Candace's hand until they joined them. When they did, he took her other hand in his, so they were facing one another.

"Have I told you how much I love you?" Candace whispered, standing on tiptoe as she spoke into his ear.

"You can tell me those words as often as you like, because I will never tire of hearing them."

"Well, I do, and I'm so glad we decided to come here."

A noise made them both look up, and Logan gave the celebrant an apologetic smile.

"Can we just skip to the part where we say I do and I get to kiss the bride?" Logan joked. "No need to waste your time doing the entire ceremony."

Everyone laughed along with him, and he dipped his head for a sneaky kiss before their informal ceremony started. For a man who thought he'd never find happiness, would always be alone, life hadn't turned out half-bad. *In the end.*

"That," Logan said, kissing her mouth, "was," another kiss, "perfect."

Candace laughed, stretching out on the sun lounger before Logan held down her arms and lay down on top of her.

"Are you referring to our wedding or the amazing food?"

"Neither. I was talking about you and me being naked in the shower."

"Logan!"

"Honey, there's a reason we checked into a private villa. No one's going to tell me off for talking dirty with my wife, especially not at the per night price we're paying."

Candace swatted at him halfheartedly, at the same time as she stretched her neck out so he could kiss her. She groaned as his tongue darted out to trail across her skin, making every part of her tingle and think about exactly what they'd been doing in the shower only a short time ago.

"What you're doing to me right now definitely needs to stay private," she said with a laugh.

His hand skimmed her body, caressing her hip and running down her thigh.

"Logan!"

He raised his head, locking eyes with her. The stare he was giving her sent a shiver down her spine, a lick of pleasure that made her push Logan back up a little so she could run her hands down his bare chest. The physical reaction she had to her husband made it hard to concentrate on anything else when he was this close, and this bare, to her. But she wanted to tell him something that she'd been waiting all afternoon to share with him.

"Logan, there's something I want to give you."

He dropped a kiss to her lips before pushing up and moving back to lie on the lounger beside hers. The sun had almost completely faded now, but lying outside their villa was just as magical in the half-light as it was during the middle of the day.

"You do remember that we agreed on no gifts, right? This vacation is more than enough, for both of us."

Candace reached beneath the lounger, her hand connecting with a small box. She pulled it out and sat up.

"I promise that it cost less than twenty dollars, so you can't complain."

Logan's eyebrows pulled together, like he was trying to figure out what she could possibly have in the box. Her heart was racing, beating a million times a minute, her eyes never leaving Logan's. She still couldn't believe what she was about to tell him.

"Well, I would have guessed a snorkel or something

for our Great Barrier dive tomorrow, but that small? Hmm."

Candace passed the little box to him, wondering if she'd gone a little overboard by putting a bow around it. Maybe she should have just told him.

"Just promise me that you won't freak out," she mumbled.

Logan squeezed her hand, looking worried, as he reached for it. She looked at how tiny the little box was in his hand as he undid the bow and slipped the lid off.

"What...?"

She held her breath, barely able to even keep her eyes open as his face froze, recognition dawning.

"Is this what I think it is?" he asked.

Candace moved to sit beside her husband as he took the white plastic stick from the box as carefully as he would hold a broken bird, his eyes never leaving it. The pink word *pregnant* was bold, not something he could miss, although she got why he might not believe it straightaway.

"Logan?" she whispered.

He finally turned, the stick still in his hand. "We're having a baby?"

Logan's voice was deep, the emotion in his voice impossible to miss as he stared at her.

"It's very early still, but yeah," she replied. "We're having a baby."

He carefully put the test back in the box and put the lid back on, before slowly turning around and holding his arms out, pulling her against him.

"We're having a baby," he whispered, his lips against

the top of her head, kissing into her hair. "We're actually going to have a baby."

"Is that okay?" she whispered back, crushed against him.

"Hell, yes, that's okay!" he exclaimed, hands on her upper arms as he pushed her back, held her at arms' length. "Honey, aside from marrying you, this is the best thing that's ever happened to me. Honestly."

"Promise?" she asked, tearing up at listening to him say the words she'd been hoping to hear.

"I promise," he said straight back, lying down and pulling her on top of him so her body covered his. "Hand on my heart, I promise."

"At least we know why I've been so darn emotional," she joked.

"Come here, Mama," he said, yanking a strand of hair to make her lean down more.

"Logan!"

"Just shut up and kiss me," he demanded. "I only have, what, eight months of you to myself? That means I'm going to be making the most of every moment before I have to share you."

Candace crushed her mouth to Logan's, kissing him like she'd been deprived of his mouth for an eternity.

"So, you'd like more of that?" she asked, loving his hot breath against her skin, before touching her lips to his again and teasing him with her tongue.

"Yes," he murmured, "God, yes."

"Well, then, Mr. Murdoch, let's not waste a minute."

Candace shut her eyes, focused only on the feel of Logan's mouth pressed to hers, his hands as they roamed up under her dress, caressing her bare skin. They were alone on one of the most beautiful islands in the world, she was with the man of her dreams and very soon they'd have a family of their own.

Life couldn't get any better than this, and if it could, she didn't care. For her, this was perfection.

* * * * *

Mills & Boon® Hardback
April 2014

ROMANCE

A D'Angelo Like No Other	Carole Mortimer
Seduced by the Sultan	Sharon Kendrick
When Christakos Meets His Match	Abby Green
The Purest of Diamonds?	Susan Stephens
Secrets of a Bollywood Marriage	Susanna Carr
What the Greek's Money Can't Buy	Maya Blake
The Last Prince of Dahaar	Tara Pammi
The Sicilian's Unexpected Duty	Michelle Smart
One Night with Her Ex	Lucy King
The Secret Ingredient	Nina Harrington
Her Soldier Protector	Soraya Lane
Stolen Kiss From a Prince	Teresa Carpenter
Behind the Film Star's Smile	Kate Hardy
The Return of Mrs Jones	Jessica Gilmore
Her Client from Hell	Louisa George
Flirting with the Forbidden	Joss Wood
The Last Temptation of Dr Dalton	Robin Gianna
Resisting Her Rebel Hero	Lucy Ryder

MEDICAL

200 Harley Street: Surgeon in a Tux	Carol Marinelli
200 Harley Street: Girl from the Red Carpet	Scarlet Wilson
Flirting with the Socialite Doc	Melanie Milburne
His Diamond Like No Other	Lucy Clark

314GEN STD HB

Mills & Boon® Large Print
April 2014

ROMANCE

Defiant in the Desert	Sharon Kendrick
Not Just the Boss's Plaything	Caitlin Crews
Rumours on the Red Carpet	Carole Mortimer
The Change in Di Navarra's Plan	Lynn Raye Harris
The Prince She Never Knew	Kate Hewitt
His Ultimate Prize	Maya Blake
More than a Convenient Marriage?	Dani Collins
Second Chance with Her Soldier	Barbara Hannay
Snowed in with the Billionaire	Caroline Anderson
Christmas at the Castle	Marion Lennox
Beware of the Boss	Leah Ashton

HISTORICAL

Not Just a Wallflower	Carole Mortimer
Courted by the Captain	Anne Herries
Running from Scandal	Amanda McCabe
The Knight's Fugitive Lady	Meriel Fuller
Falling for the Highland Rogue	Ann Lethbridge

MEDICAL

Gold Coast Angels: A Doctor's Redemption	Marion Lennox
Gold Coast Angels: Two Tiny Heartbeats	Fiona McArthur
Christmas Magic in Heatherdale	Abigail Gordon
The Motherhood Mix-Up	Jennifer Taylor
The Secret Between Them	Lucy Clark
Craving Her Rough Diamond Doc	Amalie Berlin

0314 GEN STD LP

Mills & Boon® Hardback
May 2014

ROMANCE

The Only Woman to Defy Him	Carol Marinelli
Secrets of a Ruthless Tycoon	Cathy Williams
Gambling with the Crown	Lynn Raye Harris
The Forbidden Touch of Sanguardo	Julia James
One Night to Risk it All	Maisey Yates
A Clash with Cannavaro	Elizabeth Power
The Truth About De Campo	Jennifer Hayward
Sheikh's Scandal	Lucy Monroe
Beach Bar Baby	Heidi Rice
Sex, Lies & Her Impossible Boss	Jennifer Rae
Lessons in Rule-Breaking	Christy McKellen
Twelve Hours of Temptation	Shoma Narayanan
Expecting the Prince's Baby	Rebecca Winters
The Millionaire's Homecoming	Cara Colter
The Heir of the Castle	Scarlet Wilson
Swept Away by the Tycoon	Barbara Wallace
Return of Dr Maguire	Judy Campbell
Heatherdale's Shy Nurse	Abigail Gordon

MEDICAL

200 Harley Street: The Proud Italian	Alison Roberts
200 Harley Street: American Surgeon in London	Lynne Marshall
A Mother's Secret	Scarlet Wilson
Saving His Little Miracle	Jennifer Taylor

Mills & Boon® Large Print

May 2014

ROMANCE

HISTORICAL

MEDICAL

Discover more romance at

www.millsandboon.co.uk

- ❤ WIN great prizes in our exclusive competitions
- ❤ BUY new titles before they hit the shops
- ❤ BROWSE new books and REVIEW your favourites
- ❤ SAVE on new books with the Mills & Boon® Bookclub™
- ❤ DISCOVER new authors

PLUS, to chat about your favourite reads, get the latest news and find special offers:

- 🄵 Find us on facebook.com/millsandboon
- 🐦 Follow us on twitter.com/millsandboonuk
- ❤ Sign up to our newsletter at millsandboon.co.uk